DARK REDEMPTION

AN AMERICAN MERCENARY THRILLER

JASON KASPER

Severn River
PUBLISHING

Severn River Publishing
www.SevernRiverPublishing.com

This is a work of fiction. Names, characters, businesses, places, events and incidents are either the products of the author's imagination or used in a fictitious manner. Any resemblance to actual persons, living or dead, or actual events is purely coincidental.

ISBN: 978-1-951249-50-2 (Paperback)

For information contact:

Jason@Jason-Kasper.com

Jason-Kasper.com

Be the first to learn about new releases and get free newsletter only bonus content by signing up at jason-kasper.com/newsletter

To Bryan, Dustin, Jeremiah, and LaDavid

DOL

DARK REDEMPTION

JUDGMENT

Demon est deus inversus

-A demon is a god reflected

1

January 1, 2009
The Complex
Two-hour flight from San Antonio International
Airport

I eased myself out of the pickup, taking in the view of pale, solitary desert neatly framed by open hangar doors. A security truck loaded with armed Outfit operators cruised slowly in the distance, its path a thin line between the arid expanse of sand and steep plateaus lining the bleak horizon.

The frail pitch of approaching jet engines sliced through the low murmur of men's voices echoing around me. I looked at the crowd of Outfit shooters lining the dusty white walls of the hangar, every spare member of the Handler's private army standing tensely as they awaited their first glance of his face.

I grinned to myself, but the expression was quickly

erased by the frigid winter breeze that washed into the hangar. Between being plucked from the African equator a day earlier and the hasty shower that left my hair wet, the desert outside San Antonio may as well have been the Arctic.

I barely had time to close the pickup door before Sergio accosted me from behind.

"Where the fuck have you been?" He was frowning, anxious, the gray amid his dark hair more prominent than usual.

"I had to get Bay Six ready for my mission debrief."

"He's only got ninety minutes before he has to be wheels-up again. Counting for transit on and off the compound, that leaves us an hour for your brief. Remember what I told you—"

"Professionalism. Got it."

"We've got two pickups to move him and his security detail into the compound. I'll be with him in the lead vehicle, and I want you in the trail truck."

"Okay."

"His security detail will provide all instructions. They've got tactical control from the time his jet lands until it takes off again, so we are to comply with whatever they say."

"Sure."

"This is a pivotal day for the Outfit. I expect you to conduct yourself accordingly."

"Sergio, when has my conduct been less than professional? Besides, I couldn't imagine a better way to spend New Year's Day."

His posture stiffened. "David, this is not the time—"

"My Christmas present was some hashish in Somalia, and now I'm here with you fuckers."

We heard the jet touch down on the far end of the runway. I drew a long breath to steady myself and noticed a look of fear crossing Sergio's face.

"Screw this up, David, and I'm not going to be the one making you pay. He will. But I won't have my career degraded because of your arrogance."

Forcing myself to exhale, I smiled at him. "I wouldn't worry about that. People will be talking about this debrief for years."

The booming activation of the jet's thrust reversers heralded its deceleration before we could see it through the open hangar door, and Sergio cracked the knuckles on both hands before self-consciously dropping them to his sides. "The Handler's never taken a debrief in person here before."

If the next hour went the way I intended, he never would again.

After my discharge from the Army less than a year ago, I descended into a suicidal despair. But providence led me to Boss, Matz, and Ophie, a mercenary trio that had defined my existence since our first meeting. They introduced me to Karma, the woman whose love had given me a reason to live. Since their death—and hers—at the hands of the faceless criminal mastermind I was about to meet, I was consumed by the burning, rabid desire for revenge. I knew I wouldn't survive long enough to enjoy my long-awaited victory over the Handler, but death was a foregone conclusion in my ragged pursuit of vengeance. In a way, the greatest favor he could bestow on me would be to extinguish the last flicker of life that blazed with the sole motivation of killing him. I'd embrace death so long as I could offer the same to him in return, ember for inferno.

After my brutal three-day combat mission in Somalia, I wasn't at peak physical condition for an assassination attempt. My left shoulder was strained from hauling the heavy case through a firefight with an Islamic militia, and my wrist was rubbed raw from the handcuff that had been removed only an hour ago. But there would be no second chances; I'd staged a set of scissors next to the coffeemaker in the briefing room, another beside the projector, and stocked my pockets with metal pens that could be thrust into a human eye socket with great effect.

Barring access to those tools, I'd aim to either crush his skull repeatedly with whatever hard object I could find or bite through his carotid.

"All right," Sergio said resolutely as the whooshing howl of jet engines grew louder. "Here we go."

Another gust of frigid wind disturbed the giant American flag suspended from the cross beams above us. In my mind I was suddenly on a sliver of Dominican beach with Ian as he recovered me from exile, listening to him speak the words that would ultimately send me to Africa and now here, moments away from meeting my greatest enemy.

I made contact with a source who used to work for the Handler's organization...there was a survivor from Boss's team. Whoever survived is now working for the Handler.

Recalling those words caused the same sinking feeling of dread as the first time I'd heard them. Clenching my jaw, I forced my attention back to the tarmac.

The desert plateaus beyond the hangar vanished behind the sleek white bullet of the business jet rolling into view, a sweeping red line tracing its length. I counted seven oval-shaped windows reflecting the hangar back on us, and guessed there could be no more than twenty passengers aboard, half of whom were probably his security. The plane, which had no tail number, must have originated from an airfield private enough for this conspicuous lack of identification to go unreported.

The jet coasted to a halt outside the hangar, its engines emitting an eerie, high-pitched whistle that matched the constant tone of combat-induced ringing in my ears.

I breathed in the sickly kerosene smell of jet fuel exhaust and folded my arms against the cold as a clamshell door behind the cockpit unfolded to reveal a set of stairs lowering to the tarmac. Everyone in the hangar stared fixedly at the plane, awaiting the imminent flood of bodyguards.

Instead, a single figure appeared in the doorway.

The silhouette stood stock-still for a moment, and then descended the stairs with a certain lithe grace. After setting foot on the ground, the figure unhurriedly approached us, empty-handed and unaccompanied.

It was a woman.

She may have been many things, but I could tell from her appearance that she was definitely not a bodyguard. Her long red hair drifted in the wind, offset by a conservative knee-length skirt and short heels.

I looked to Sergio for guidance, but his eyes were turned to her, his lips slightly parted. I couldn't tell if he recognized her.

As she approached us, she didn't spare so much as a sideways glance to the security vehicles posted beyond the compound fence or the rows of Complex operators filling the hangar behind us.

Instead, her relaxed gaze was fixed on me until she stopped a few feet away. Her features held a peculiar fairness, a delicate grace beset by the cool reserve of her gunmetal gray eyes that remained composed and busi-nesslike.

"Mr. Rivers, are you ready?"

"Absolutely."

She lifted a hand toward the plane. "Good. He's waiting for you."

In a split second, it all made sense.

Why wouldn't the Handler remain on his jet? He'd be unseen and protected within the comfort of his usual travel accommodations, safely parked amid the Complex's concentric security rings.

Perfect. This would bring me even closer to him than I'd hoped.

Sergio was the first to blink.

"The brief was to take place in the planning bay, Sage," he blurted. "His aide gave me very specific instructions."

"And yet the Handler has chosen to receive the brief on his plane."

Sergio's mouth opened before he swallowed and said, "Very well. Let's go."

"We would prefer you supervise security until his jet has taken off."

"I have a man in charge of that."

Sage flashed him a mischievous grin. "You have some-thing to add to the debrief?"

"David is my recruit. I should be present."

"You can have Mr. Rivers back when the Handler is done with him. You've already blown one chance, Sergio. You're not getting another."

Though he said nothing, his eyes didn't move from hers.

"Well," I said, breaking the silence that had fallen

between them, "the Handler probably wants to hear all about Africa. Probably shouldn't keep him waiting."

I took a step toward the jet, but Sage looked to me coldly. "Remove everything from your person and empty the contents of your pockets completely. Phone, pens, paper. His security staff has a pronounced tendency to react poorly to any items they find."

Sergio held out his hand.

I slapped my work phone, wallet, and battered notepad into his waiting palm, then reluctantly added the metal pens to the tally.

"That's it," I said.

Sage shook her head. "Your wristwatch, Mr. Rivers."

I unstrapped it and handed it to Sergio, the intensity of his glare displaying one final concentrated effort to impart his earnestness upon me. "Represent the Outfit, David."

"I plan on it."

Sage said, "After you, Mr. Rivers."

I walked toward the lowered stairs of the plane. The click of her heels followed me across the tarmac before all was lost in the dreamlike, white noise cry of the idling jet. Its horizontal crimson stripe turned to blood before me, a lucid reminder of my impending confrontation.

I didn't feel myself ascending the staircase. A thousand aches and pains from my fight for survival in Africa were left on the ground as I floated upward, my body weightless from the magnitude of meeting the Handler face-to-face at last. The crescendo of the engines died as I entered the soundproofed cabin and turned my eyes to a long interior divided into segments by partially open doors.

I crossed through a lounge filled with black leather

couches offset by cream surfaces, my shadow whispering past a glossy wood partition as I entered the center of the cabin. Looking past an unoccupied conference table flanked by blank flat screens, I saw a final sliding door blocking my view of the aft section of the plane.

I advanced toward the tail, my heart slamming as I slid open the door. A low couch stretched across one wall, while opposite it two seats faced each other. The windows were opaque, allowing in ambient light while blocking any outside view.

The room was empty.

I whirled around as Sage entered behind me. "Where is he?"

Her eyes creased in an otherwise imperceptible smile. "He's not coming here, Mr. Rivers. You're going to him."

* * *

After barreling down the runway at a greater speed than any aircraft I'd ever flown in, we swiftly rose to a cruising altitude I couldn't estimate through the opaque windows and soared for hours with no means to gauge how much time had elapsed since our departure. As we finally began our descent to places unknown, the cabin of the plane was completely silent.

And that's what was most unsettling about the entire experience—not Sage sealing me into the aft section of the plane without a word, or being forced to spend so many hours between a locked door and a lavatory. Even the unknown destination took second place to the silence of my surroundings, the expansive smells of the desert I'd just left replaced by richly conditioned leather and plush carpet, a tomb that allowed the high-pitch ring of my permanent hearing loss to surface with perfect clarity. The ringing became a soundtrack to my mind's churning through a cast of characters now reduced to memories in an intricate web of lies I'd built around myself to get closer to the Handler.

I remembered watching Ophie torture a man named Luka in the basement of our team house. *We know you killed Caspian. You're just here to answer for it.* Before his gruesome death, Luka had screamed over and over that the Iranian, not he, had been responsible for the murder.

But when I asked who the Iranian was, Matz had curtly responded, *He's dead already. Stop talking.*

In the wake of my team's massacre, I had returned from a brief exile in the Dominican Republic to meet Ian's contact from the Handler's organization, a heavyset Indian man who had told me in no uncertain terms that I was about to meet the survivor from Boss's team. The man had also gotten me a job interview for the Outfit and, most importantly, provided the words *Khasham Khada* that would eventually save my life.

A month later I'd met Sergio, who oversaw my conduct in the test that would determine my admission into the Outfit.

The test had nearly killed me. Actually, it *had* killed me, though my drowning in the frigid waters of a winter harbor had been erased when a carefully staged medical team had resuscitated me. After a lengthy psychiatric evaluation, I'd attended my first job interview for the Outfit, and was then paired with an experienced partner named Jais for my debut mission.

The mission was simple: link up with a recovery team, meet with an old woman referred to as the Silver Widow, and take possession of a case. But after fighting our way across the war-torn wilderness of southern Somalia, Jais and I had barely escaped an enemy militia to reach our link-up site. The recovery team transported us to a hidden structure, separating me from Jais.

I had been summoned to meet the Silver Widow alone, and instead of an old woman, I found the face of a young, beautiful Somali woman behind a headdress of interlocking silver pieces. And in that dreamlike exchange, the woman told me that she knew I wanted to kill the Handler, and sought the same end. Her instructions were simple enough, but if I failed to follow them exactly, she warned I'd be killed before my first sunset in America. That sunset was now a few hours away, and her words weighed heavily on my mind.

I heard the precise click of a lock neatly opening, followed by the cabin door sliding sideways.

Sage stood in the doorway, her red hair neatly parted, tucked behind an unadorned ear on one side and descending in wavy lengths past her chin. Shale eyes flicked to the bottle of water in the cup holder beside me, then to the galley tucked in the corner.

"Why, Mr. Rivers," she said in surprise, "you haven't touched the bar."

"No."

"Given your psych evaluation, that took considerable restraint."

She'd read my file. My thoughts flickered back to the psychiatrist who had interviewed me as I tried out for the Outfit, his ice-blue eyes fixed upon mine as he dismantled my carefully maintained exterior of normalcy.

I shrugged. "It didn't take that much restraint. Not one bottle of bourbon on the plane, Sage? So much for an organization with unlimited resources."

She moved to the seat across from me, expensive-smelling perfume wafting around her as she slowly crossed one leg over the other.

"When I transport someone to meet him for the first time, they look like they're on the way to a promotion interview. But not you, Mr. Rivers."

I self-consciously rubbed my cheek. The last time I shaved was a week earlier to ensure my oxygen mask would seal to my face before the high-altitude jump into Somalia.

"I didn't have much time to clean up."

"I don't mean your appearance. I mean your eyes. You look like a man being marched to the gallows."

"Am I?"

"Maybe. Why did you get summoned to meet him?"

I examined the strangely attractive lay of her face. From one angle she appeared old enough to be my mother, but with a slight turn of her head, she looked twenty years younger.

"I don't know," I said, glancing at the opaque window next to me. "Where are we headed?"

"An airport. How many missions have you done for the Outfit?"

"One."

"What did it require?"

The recovery of a case, I thought, that I later found out contained a billet of highly enriched uranium plucked from the black market by the Handler himself. My mind danced to the mission's end, when I confronted Jais with the truth I'd pieced together from the fragments of conversations I'd overheard since becoming a criminal mercenary.

You said we'd only be outgunned as long as we were miss-

ing. The last person who told me that was Matz. I worked with him, and Boss, and Ophie. And Karma. None of them survived that day, and yet there's a survivor. That's how I know who you are...You had already left by the time I met them. They didn't call you Jais; they called you Caspian.

My partner's response to the accusation still rang painfully in my head. *They were pushing it too far, David... They wouldn't let me leave. I had to make them think I was dead.*

I met Sage's eyes. "I'll tell you all about it at the debrief. Unless it will just be me and him?"

She smiled. "Not a chance. Why aren't your team-mates from the mission with you?"

I was again transported back to the hilltop with Caspian. *I watched Ophie torture Luka to death for killing you...Luka kept saying it wasn't him, that the Iranian killed you. That was your scout, wasn't it? In the desert I asked if Sergio recruited you. You said it was an Iranian named Roshan.*

A chill ran down my spine as I replied, "There were only two of us."

In my mind, Caspian was limping toward me, forcing my hand. My last words to him were a promise that I was going to kill the Handler.

Then I shot him four times, once for each of the team-mates he had betrayed.

"And?" she asked.

After he'd fallen, I gave him one final bullet. For me.

I replied, "My partner is dead."

She drew in a long breath before her face relaxed into a self-satisfied grin. "I understand."

"You understand what?"

She didn't answer. Instead, she watched me absently

as I waited for her response, processing something behind the closed doors of her mind.

Rising soundlessly from her seat, she slipped through the doorway and slid the door back in place, the silence of the cabin punctuated by a single click of the lock re-engaging.

I raced through a mental summary of our exchange, trying to make some sense of her questions and intentions. How much did she know? How much had I revealed? Before I could consider it for more than a minute, the plane lifted slightly and then hit hard on a runway.

I flew halfway out of my seat before catching myself as the cabin's silence was broken by the screeching rumble of thrust reversers, wheel brakes, and wind resistance against the groaning aircraft frame. I braced myself with strained arms and legs for a full twenty seconds before everything went quiet once again.

I fell back into my chair with a grunt as the jet easily transitioned to a gentle forward roll. We reached a near-complete stop, and the nose of the plane veered left and then carved a neat circle in place before halting altogether. I heard the mechanical whirring of the airstair lowering, followed by hushed voices and the sound of approaching footsteps.

"Mr. Rivers," a man's voice called from the other side of the cabin door. "You are now under advanced security protocol, and any failure to comply with my instructions will be treated as a threat. Do you understand?"

His tone was as professional as a hotel concierge, and he spoke in a crisp British accent.

"Yes," I replied. "I understand."

"Face the closed lavatory door. Stand with your feet shoulder-width apart, arms straight out to your sides, hands open with palms facing down."

I rose and turned away from the voice, doing as he said. "I've assumed the position."

The click of the lock sounded behind me, and I sensed a man entering.

"Remain still until directed otherwise, eyes straight ahead."

The squared point of a black metal detector wand appeared beside my face and swept over my head before tracking around my entire body.

Once finished, the man slid a pair of goggles over my eyes. The lenses were completely blacked out, and the elastic strap fit snugly against the back of my head. My last sight before the black veil blinded me was of the lavatory door's glossy wooden veneer.

"Lower your hands to your sides, then turn to face my voice."

I complied, shuffling in a circle, and almost immediately felt the cool clasp of metal handcuffs around my wrists as they were bound in front of me. Then the man's hands encircled my sides, routing a chain behind the small of my back. He pulled the chain snug around my waist, binding my handcuffs to the restraint belt with a series of tugs and metallic clicks.

"Move forward, Mr. Rivers."

He pulled me forward by my cuffs, and as I walked to the front of the plane, a second man's gloved hand gripped the back of my neck from behind. The sound of the idling jet engines grew louder—we were approaching the open door—and just before the smell of jet exhaust sliced through the air, I caught a whiff of Sage's perfume.

I turned my head toward the scent and pulled at the restraint belt but found no more than a few inches of slack at my maximum range of motion. So I waved with one hand and called out, "I think I'll miss you most of all, Sage."

"Turn left," the man instructed, and as I did so a blast of icy air hit me. Curt commands guided me down the airstair and onto an unseen tarmac, one hand still on my neck and another now on my right triceps, guiding me from behind.

"Step down."

"Flat ground."

"Walk forward."

I walked along the pavement, my muscles tensing against an air temperature that must have been in the thirties. Burning jet exhaust gave way to moist air clean with altitude and muddled with the heavy scent of pine, and the temperature seemed below freezing. As the sound of the plane grew quieter, I could hear the footsteps of at least four people falling in a steady cadence around me.

The British man said, "Everything from the time you left the Complex until you return to it is classified. You are not to speak of it again, under any circumstances."

"I'm in the habit of keeping it to myself when I've been blindfolded and chained up by strange men."

"Anyone who asks about your time here, even the smallest details, is to be reported to your Outfit chain of command immediately. Failure to do so at the earliest opportunity is considered evidence of treason."

I gave a low, respectful whistle. "Just treason, or would that be considered, like, *high* treason?"

We came to a stop, and a second voice said, "David Rivers by direct request. Negative metal, restrained by 629."

I felt myself beginning to shiver. "I'm just trying to figure out if punishment would be the king's gallows or being hanged by the neck. Is it as bad as trading with the pirates and American colonies?"

A beep, a door handle clacking open, and I was led indoors—no pine, just warm air and the smell of metal and smooth plastic surfaces—before we passed back into the cold and I heard the rattle of a chain-link gate sliding open. As I stepped onto a softer surface, the ground shook with the roar of the jet throttling down the runway.

Then I heard the clanking of a second gate closing just behind me as I inhaled deeply through my nostrils: resinous pine, mountain air, though not the familiar low-altitude humidity of the Smokies that I would have recognized at once from a dozen hiking trips.

Pacific Northwest?

The British voice said, "I strongly advise steering clear of humor when you meet him."

"His loss. I've got a ton of Revolutionary War material—" I stumbled on a stair to my front, and a set of hands caught me from behind.

"Step up," the voice said.

I recovered my balance and walked up three stairs.

We passed into the mercifully warm interior of a building and a door clanged shut behind me. The metallic echo ringing around us sounded like a bank vault, probably reinforced against breaching, and I caught a whiff of gun oil. Hushed voices whispered on either side of me as another door opened and I was led around a turn and down a corridor.

Another halt as the voice said, "Lock-out clear."

The response came from a radio speaker above us. "*Proceed.*"

We entered another room, and the jangle of chains ended as I was stopped in place. I felt leg irons being clasped around my ankles.

Feet scuffled on smooth tile as the men around me moved into some preordained configuration. I sniffed; the scent of antiseptic was faintly discernable in the stale air around me. Then another door opened and closed to my front, and a solitary set of footsteps echoed off the tile.

A new voice, this one distinctly Southern and as genteel as a plantation owner, said, "Any problems?"

The Brit behind me responded, "None at all."

A set of hands tugged gently at my handcuffs, then the leg irons, inspecting that my restraints were properly applied.

"This'll do," the Southern voice said. "Have your team stand by outside. Shouldn't take long."

A group of footsteps departed behind me, the door slamming closed as they left.

The door to my front opened again and the Southerner called, "Whenever you're ready, sir."

"You don't have to call me sir," I said.

He gave a quiet, rapid-fire chuckle, then leaned in beside me and whispered, "I like you, boy, but you got about three seconds to put yourself right with the Lord."

I heard him step back, and for a moment I thought I detected murmuring voices somewhere in the distance before they went silent and a new set of footsteps echoed off the walls in front of me. Their methodical, rhythmic beat grew louder with each step, and between the footfalls and the ringing in my ears I could've sworn that the Southerner's breathing quickened. My own heart rate grew faster, thumping to a fever pitch as my pulse slammed in my head.

The footsteps turned a corner, then came to a stop inches away as I inhaled a clove-like incense smell in the seconds before he touched me. My circulatory system was in overdrive, manifesting all the physiological effects of a crisis situation as I stood unbearably still: chained, shackled, and unable to show the increasing panic that I felt.

Fingertips grazed my scalp, pinching to a close around my temples and sliding the elastic band of my goggles over the back of my head.

* * *

His eyes were amber.

Lucid golden pupils fixed on mine, the stare piercing through the room's bright lighting as my vision adjusted.

Blinking to gain perspective, I took in his face for the first—and very likely last—time in my life.

Short, thick eyebrows cast his amber eyes into black shadow with the slightest movement of his forehead. A Roman nose skewed to the right—perhaps one bad break in the past, or maybe several—and was set within a long, gaunt face. His skin was dark but not enough to identify a heritage—he could have been Native or Latin American, Indian or North African, Middle Eastern or Mediterranean. In his sixties, if he'd aged well, fifties if he hadn't, but certainly not outside those parameters. His head was shaved down to salt-and-pepper stubble.

His face receded and lifted from view, and I realized

he'd been leaning down to meet my eyes. He was lean and rangy: over six feet, with long, slender arms that ended in spiderlike hands.

One of them set upon my shoulder, the touch of those spindly fingers sending a flurry of chills up my spine and making the breath catch in my throat.

"David, welcome back from Africa." His voice had one of those indiscernibly foreign accents, somewhere between South African and European, that I couldn't narrow down any further. "Thank you for retrieving my case."

"It was my pleasure," I said, resuming my breathing and swallowing hard. I looked past him at the tiled walls of my surroundings, everything silvery and spotless. "Nice to meet you at last."

"Proceed with your debrief." He held the blacked-out goggles to his side, and a third man in the room stepped forward to take them.

My eyes darted sideways to assign a face to the Southerner, who was now putting the goggles into his pocket. He was a stout man wearing an open-collared dress shirt over a black canvas belt that supported a row of inverted magazines. The opposite hip bore a holstered racegun: a 1911 modified to the extent that only a professional-grade competitive shooter could come close to utilizing its full capabilities. Barrel extension, reflex sight, and a double-stack, high-capacity magazine indicating it was chambered in 9mm or .40 cal.

I looked back to the Handler, whose hands were folded to his front. Then I confidently began, "Our plane hit a storm over the Kenya-Somalia border—"

"I am familiar with the particulars," he said, nodding graciously. "So tell me what has escaped me thus far."

"I've been assured that nothing escapes you."

He spoke with the slow, patient cadence of wisdom. "Your partner placed a distress call stating that you were both surrounded by an overwhelming force of enemy fighters."

"That's correct."

"My recovery team reported that they arrived to find your partner dead and no enemy in sight." His face shuddered slightly, as if he found the contradiction distasteful. "Surely you can explain this dissonance?"

"Before we were overrun, he told me two words to use as a last resort."

"Which were what, exactly?"

"*Khasham Khada.*"

He inhaled through his nostrils. "And then your partner was killed?"

"We were both knocked unconscious in the mortar attack. I woke up to the sound of him being shot, and then I yelled the words."

"Foot soldiers don't know the meaning of *Khasham Khada*, I believe. Who did you yell these words to, David?"

"Their commander."

"Whose name was...?"

"Sasa."

The Handler nodded deeply, assuming a tight smile as if I had mentioned an old friend. "A 62-year-old Yemeni Al Qaeda operations officer not known for his compassion who was leading a platoon-sized element of fighters to personally oversee the recovery of the case. You must have quite the bluff."

"My options were limited. I played the only card I had."

"And lived to tell about it. Well done, David. But"—he hesitated—"this brings two complications to mind."

"Which are?"

"First, the nature of what you now know, but shouldn't. *Khasham Khada* itself is a simple phrase, a variation of the Farsi expression for 'wrath of God.' But in this context, David, it is one of the last vestiges of an ancient code of honor. Any aggression once those words are invoked represents a declaration of war against my Organization."

"I didn't speak it to anyone but the enemy trying to steal your case. Ask Sergio if you don't believe me—I told him I would only discuss the specifics of my survival with you, in person."

His chin was tucked low as he spoke, a slight tremor of movement in his head. "The authority to declare war on my behalf is an authority reserved for my highest envoys. Your excursion into Somalia did not grant you status as my direct representative, and yet you spoke the words anyway."

"If I hadn't, you wouldn't have the case."

"No one is disputing that. But this brings us to the second complication in this matter of ours."

"Which is?"

"There is no possibility that your late partner could have known the words *Khasham Khada*."

I felt my lungs constrict. "I don't know how he knew, but the fact that I'm alive right now is proof that he did."

The Handler didn't respond. Instead, he seemed to be contemplating some philosophical question, the focus of his eyes shifting to some grander matter than the petty affair in which he currently found himself engaged.

"Tell me," he said abruptly, "about the storm."

"The storm?"

"The one that altered the flight path of your infiltration into Somalia."

I stammered, "It, ah, was violent. A lot of turbulence. We were knocked down a few times before the emergency bailout."

"And yet you exited the plane anyway."

"We had no choice. The pilots had found a clear path, and we freefell between storm clouds."

"It seemed terrifying, didn't it?"

"It had my full attention at the time."

"Good." He nodded. "Very good, indeed. Now take a walk with me, David."

He turned his back to me and walked out the door to my front. Racegun's left hand immediately clamped onto the back of my arm, and he guided me forward with his non-gun side.

We rounded a corner to find a short hallway with three doors on the wall to my left. The middle one was open, and the Handler approached it as he continued speaking.

"The terror of the storm is a uniquely human phenomenon, David. You see, we are but transient life forms perceiving a greater terror in the sky above us."

As I was shuffled forward in my leg irons, I decided that this guy was even more insane than I'd thought. I followed him into a room built like a giant shower, with tiled walls and a floor beset by a large circular drain.

The primary fixture inside was a throne of sorts—a high-backed, utilitarian chair of thick golden wood segments arranged into uncomfortable right angles and situated at the dead center of the room.

In it sat a paunchy Indian man restrained by leather straps at his ankles, chest, wrist, and lap, his head shaved into an awkward buzz cut and topped with a metal cap that was strapped around his jaw. From the top of this metallic crown emerged a long, writhing red snake of a cable running down his side and behind the chair. The Indian man was sweating heavily, and he looked at me with deep-set eyes that I recognized at once.

He was my fellow conspirator from the Redwood forest the year before, which now seemed a lifetime away.

"Who is he?" I asked, hoping my question came before a pause could give me away.

Ignoring my question, the Handler simply continued speaking, untouched by the macabre sight we'd just stumbled upon. "But to the eternal—to nature—storms purify, enrich; they replenish the earth with an order that seems chaotic until understood as part of the sum total of life."

I cleared my throat uneasily, trying to continue the dialogue against a rising swell of fear. "The healing qualities of the storm weren't the first thing that came to mind as I was freefalling through lightning toward a million bad guys."

"A lightning storm. How appropriate to our current situation."

"How so?"

"Lightning only appears with imbalance. The volatility of a storm cloud causes it to gain a negative electrical charge. But the universe is interconnected, so the ground beneath the storm becomes positively charged in return. Nature's response is lightning. An instantaneous flash, hotter than the surface of the sun, containing a billion volts of electricity moving at three hundred million kilometers per hour, and yet representing the ultimate symbol of harmony. The ability to maintain harmony creates true power. In nature, and in human affairs."

"Who is this man?" I repeated.

"Upraj Raza Sukhija," the Handler said, somewhat sadly. Then he placed a hand on my shoulder and addressed the Indian. "I believe I have one of yours here beside me—David Clayton Rivers."

The last threads of my deception had finally unraveled to their inevitable conclusion, and yet with my hands bound to the chain encircling my waist, I was utterly helpless to act. Of course I was, I thought. The Handler wasn't in the habit of being reckless with his safety.

I watched the Indian. Was he about to crack?

Had he already?

But the Indian shook his head to the extent possible within his restraints, speaking quietly with his jaw limited by the leather strap. "I am afraid I have disappointed you once more. This is not one of mine."

The Handler released my shoulder. "I think he is. We had an amenable arrangement, Upraj. I pretended to believe you dead, and you funneled would-be assassins to the Outfit in the hopes that one would kill me someday. But you finally overstepped your bounds with this recruit. You told him of *Khasham Khada*, didn't you?"

"I have told many. But I do not know this young man, so do not let my guilt cloud your judgment."

"I did so enjoy your aggressive recruiting efforts for my warrior caste. So long as I never visited the Complex, there was no reason for me to stop you. But I must, dear brother, draw the line. At. You...COMPROMISING"—he shouted this single word so loudly that I jumped beside him, but his voice returned to its low cadence after a slight pause—"what was once a shared code of honor."

The Indian's response was spoken with an increasing

quaver of fear. "The greatest honor of all would be succeeding in having you killed."

"Look at me now, David." The Handler lowered his eyes to mine, the amber tint of his irises dotted with gold flecks as he drew close. "Speak the truth. Do you know this man?"

Behind him, I could see the Indian watching me closely. And in that moment, the weight of the entire world descended upon my shoulders, my every action from the night I met Boss's team to slaying Caspian to my present situation compressing in a split-second response.

I smiled. "He's strapped to an electric chair, and I'm in handcuffs. Pretty sure I'm gonna go with 'never seen him before' no matter what. But the truth is"—I turned my gaze to the perspiring Indian, who stared at me in return —"if I'd seen this man so much as once before today, I'd be sweating bullets worse than he is."

I met the Handler's stare again, gazing coolly into the fiery depths of his eyes, which were now watching me for any sign of deception. Lowering my voice and leaning my face toward his, I continued, "Do I look like I'm sweating bullets?"

The Handler continued to watch me, the vaguely discernible tremor in his head increasing until his face contorted into a momentary grimace.

And then he began to laugh.

It started as a slight chortle and then extended into long, rolling bursts of laughter that echoed in the chamber. I turned to my side. "How about it, Racegun? Do I look scared to you?"

Racegun said nothing. I could tell this wasn't the first time he'd been a witness to whatever was about to transpire in the death chamber. Judging by his disturbed expression, though, he wasn't any more thrilled to be present than I was, and that single fact frightened me as much as everything else I'd seen put together.

The Handler's laughter came to an unhurried end, and he rubbed under his eye with index and middle fingers joined. I looked back at him and shrugged. "You want to fry this guy, that's your prerogative. But don't do it on my account."

He sighed helplessly. "I suppose it is possible that the code has spread beyond my attempts to contain it. So I'm not going to 'fry' him, David."

The Handler turned his stare back to me, the lines of his face falling long and straight save the angled bridge of his nose. "You are."

My eyebrows shot up. "Excuse me?"

The Handler nodded to Racegun, who approached me and inserted a key into the lock connecting my handcuffs to the chain restraint belt. After freeing my hands, he stepped back, leaving me with a clear line of sight to the Handler, who gestured to the wall beside me. Beside a red telephone unit was a switch box with a long, Y-shaped assembly emerging, its handle canted toward the floor.

I remembered the young Somali woman's words: *If the opportunity to kill him seems certain, then do not proceed.*

I was still handcuffed, but it would only take one violent impact of the back of his skull into the concrete floor to kill him if I was lucky; two or more if I wasn't. Either way, his death would only take seconds.

He is going to test you, and when the moment seems perfect to complete your revenge, that is the very time you must not do it.

If ever I was facing a test, it was now.

I turned to him and said, "He's done nothing to me."

"If you do not obey my command, then the next body in the chair will be yours."

I shook my head grimly and replied, before considering the consequences, "I don't murder innocent people."

The Handler smiled. "As you wish, David Rivers."

Racegun grabbed me from behind, wrenching my arms back to immobilize me and rotating me sideways until I saw nothing but the sweating Indian's paunchy frame tied to the chair, his eyes wild with fear.

The Handler pressed a button beside the switch, then raised his voice above the low, churning howl of an exhaust fan that activated in the ceiling. "You see, my friend, I am the storm cloud that terrifies those below while replenishing life." He rested his fingertips on the handle of the switch. "And like the storm, I correct imbalances with a sudden... surge... of... *power.*"

The Indian chanted, "Life begins when you are absolutely free—"

The Handler threw the switch upward. A deep booming sound was followed by the sizzling hiss of an electrical current.

The Indian's body convulsed and strained against the restraints before freezing in place.

His expression was inhuman, eyes bulging so much that I was certain one or both would burst from their socket. I watched his skin turn from earthen brown to a horrid crimson, his face swollen and warped as a froth of bloody vomit spilled down his chin. More horrendous was the grotesque smell that filled the room—burning hair and smoking flesh congealing into a repulsive stench as horrid as any of the decomposing corpses I'd pulled guard duty beside in the invasion of Iraq.

The Handler flipped the switch back and the Indian's

body slumped forward, stock-still, as if turned to stone by the jolt.

Releasing his hand from the switch, the Handler gestured to the man's ghastly remains.

"David," he said kindly, "the throne is yours."

I threw my head back and felt it impact Racegun's skull, but before I could resist further he swung me down effortlessly. My shoulder bounced hard off the ground, and I looked up to see him withdrawing a leather sap from his belt before bringing it down over my head with the grace and force of a pro golf swing. The pummeling impact against my head barely registered before my world turned to darkness.

I awoke to the sting of liquid against a tender welt on the side of my head, followed by the cool trickle of water pouring down my face. I realized, somewhat abruptly and with a chilling stab of fear, that it was coming from a sponge being pressed against my bare scalp.

They'd shaved my head.

I opened my eyes as a strap was tightened around my chin, pinning the sponge against the top of my head by way of the same metal cap that had served as the Indian's final crown. Jerking my limbs, I found them already restrained by straps pinning me to the chair by wrists, ankles, lap, and chest. The sensation of the leather bindings mixed with the wet sponge on my head was enough to rile me into a near panic.

I felt a sudden twinge of regret for passing on my only chance to attack the Handler before I was strapped to the chair, but did I ever really have that chance?

"David." The Handler stepped in front of me. "Tell me what the Silver Widow said to you. Her exact words, if you please."

Even if the Handler somehow knew everything about my past, he couldn't be aware of one fact—I'd never met the Silver Widow. I had revealed to no one that a young Somali woman had summoned me instead and told me exactly how to lie about the meeting.

You will tell them you met with a very old woman.

She did not remove her mask.

She did not speak.

Unless, of course, the Somali woman worked for him. Was this another test, orchestrated to assess my integrity under the most severe pressure? The Handler would certainly be capable of it. Either way, he was judging my response, and the wrong one would get me electrocuted.

I spoke in a low murmur with the strap under my jaw. "Why do you need to know about the Silver Widow?"

He spun toward the wall and raised his hand for the switch but halted as I replied quickly, "She didn't speak."

His hand lowered. He turned back to me, nostrils flaring, his face a volatile storm that unnerved me. But his voice was as placid as ever.

"Describe her to me, please."

I fumbled for the right words, settling for, "She never removed her mask. But she was old. Frail."

"You received the case immediately?"

"No. She made me smoke something from a pipe."

"Smoke what, David?"

"I don't know. I saw things."

"A vision?"

"Yes."

"David, what did you see?"

"My end."

He screamed again, his voice a roar against the concrete walls, "What did you *SEE?*"

I waited for the echo of his words to evaporate before saying, "I put a .454 revolver in my mouth and blew my head off."

The Handler looked away from me, the veins in his forehead receding into a mask of dignity once more. He stared at the wall behind me, his face contemplative, almost meditative, as he absorbed my words.

He stroked the side of his face, tapping an index finger against it three times before speaking. "It would seem the Silver Widow has saved your life, David. I need you for a mission. One that, unlike your last endeavor on my behalf, *is* under my direct protection."

"You have another case to recover?"

"In a way. Your role is to protect my envoy."

I looked to Racegun, then back at the Handler. "It would seem you're not suffering from a lack of bodyguards."

"Just so. But I need a guardian angel. Fail at that"—his voice was slow, methodical—"and allow any harm to come to my ambassador, and there is no intervention on this blue marble of ours that will keep your heart beating. You've faced death before, but never so agonizingly as I can offer it to you. Trust me when I say the chair in which you sit is the utmost mercy you'll find me capable of. If my envoy returns alive, you and I will meet again under more agreeable circumstances. I give you my word on that."

I didn't doubt he was telling the truth. And at that next meeting, I would die.

But only after I killed him.

In that moment, I didn't know how I'd be able to

achieve his death—I would figure that out only in the days to follow, and under the most unusual of circumstances—but my singular thought was, *Our next meeting is the last one for both of us, fucker.*

I replied, "I look forward to it."

A deep bow of his head. "Godspeed, David Rivers. Do not fail me."

He strolled out of the room. Racegun approached, unhooking the leather strap from beneath my chin and pulling the metal cap off my head. The wet sponge fell to the floor with a sickening *plop* as he pulled the blacked-out goggles from his pocket, and I used my last second of sight to steal another glance at the modified 1911 on his hip. I saw the edge of a ported slide emerging from the holster before he affixed the goggles over my eyes and stretched the elastic strap backward, letting it snap hard against the back of my skull.

"You know," I said, "that's one hell of a gun."

He replied with two words, his Southern accent every bit as polished as it had been before watching the Indian get electrocuted.

"I know."

Then I heard him walk into the hall, a final snap of his fingers cracking off the tiled walls as he followed the sound of the Handler's departing steps.

REDEEMER

Sua Sponte

-Of their own accord

2

"Double Woodford on the rocks," a woman said.

The sleeve of a blue service uniform took the empty glass beside me and set down a new one.

"You're an angel," I said to her, fishing another $100 bill from my pocket.

In the course of making travel arrangements that included the procurement of a new passport with my real name, the Handler's people had given me a generous stipend. I had no intention of returning change.

A far better use of the money was purchasing a one-time access pass at the priciest airport lounge I could find by my gate and tipping generously enough on my initial glass of bourbon that I wouldn't have to sit at the bar and interact with the loafer-wearing business elite in order to drink. I'd quickly reached a verbal arrangement with the server, and then retired to a comfortable, secluded seat facing a tall window and the overcast view of the Pacific

Northwest. Unbuttoning my suit jacket, I stared into the mist, drinking alone.

"How much time do I have?" I asked as the bartender began walking away.

"Forty minutes to boarding."

"Let's do a refill in fifteen."

"Certainly, sir."

Then, reconsidering, I called after her, "Life is short. Let's make it ten."

I lifted the new glass and sniffed the surface of the dark liquid. Then I took a sip, welcoming another wave of slow, rolling warmth spreading throughout my chest. Lowering the glass to my lap, I closed my eyes again.

And, as had been the case since his bodyguards escorted me out of our meeting, I saw the Handler's face.

From what I knew of him and his procedures, there was no question that his mind and reputation alone had compelled countless trained killers to do his will in a war that only he understood. Based on what I'd personally witnessed at home and abroad, his operations blurred the lines between military and criminal, murderous and political. But in the brief span of our meeting, he'd swung from total poise to complete rage, from casually threatening my execution to demanding my obedience on a mission of his choosing, its relevance to my own situation beyond my comprehension.

You couldn't reason with such instability, I decided— you could only kill it, or be killed by it. No other outcome seemed possible, save a temporary alliance that might forestall one of the previous two alternatives.

Whatever made him interrogate me about the Silver Widow had been of strategic import. But judging by his cryptic farewell I had no doubts I would die at our next meeting.

The only question: could I kill him first?

By my best estimate, the flight from the Handler's airstrip to Seattle had taken two hours, but between the jet's speed and the opaque windows, I still knew nothing about the location of his compound. They could have launched me halfway down the Pacific Coast or flown me in circles for half the trip.

A man spoke beside me.

"When the sky's clear, you can see Mount Rainier out that window."

I opened my eyes to see a hand gesturing to my front, holding a glass of something clear and carbonated. Directing my gaze back to the tall window, I saw a depthless expanse of white cloud against dull tarmac, luggage trucks, and taxiing aircraft.

I lifted my glass and took another sip of bourbon. "I'll keep that in mind during the three days a year that Seattle gets a clear sky."

"The sky might be clearing sooner than you think, David."

I jerked my head sideways, looking past the lapels of a navy suit jacket to a lean face devoid of its usual thin glasses. The man's eyes reflected a smug sense of amusement.

"Jesus, Ian," I said in a low, disbelieving voice. "You need to get the fuck out of here. Now."

Ian gracefully leaned a small carry-on bag against the chair beside me, then took a seat and crossed a loafer over the opposite knee.

My throat tightened with panic as I considered the implications of his appearance. What was he doing here

—and with the Indian dead, how could Ian have possibly found me?

Was he a deep cover agent for the Handler?

He sipped his drink, the ice cubes softly clinking together. "You're safe until you step foot outside the Sky Club; I've got an informant monitoring your surveillance."

"Who's your informant?"

"The Indian gave me direct contact with his inside man. That's how I knew your flight information—"

"The Indian's dead."

Ian took another sip. "Then handing off his source seems a prudent measure."

I rubbed my forehead in disbelief at his nonchalance. "The Indian's dead because the inside source burned him. Your source is a double agent."

"He's not. You're alive and being employed at a higher level than before."

"Ian, I'm burned. I've already been interrogated once. You weren't mentioned, but it's only a matter of time before he discovers your involvement."

"It's a game of risk, David. We're going to finish this thing. By the way, you trying to make me feel better about going bald? What's up with the haircut?"

He was gazing at my head in a nonjudgmental way, analyzing my fresh, unwanted buzz cut.

He didn't realize what we were up against, hadn't listened to Caspian describe how the Handler knew exactly where we'd been hiding all along.

But there was no explaining that to him. We didn't have the time, this certainly wasn't the place, and, beneath it all, I no longer knew if I could trust him. There were too many coincidences to rule out Ian's complicity with the Handler. A few minutes earlier, my confidence that Ian wasn't a deep cover agent was 60/40 at best. His sudden appearance dropped my calculus to 50/50, and I couldn't explain that to him either.

Instead, I muttered, "I think the Handler knows everything."

"Don't give me that. I've got the situation under control."

"Really—like you had the survivor from Boss's team under control?"

I immediately regretted the words.

Ian lit up with the prospect of additional information. "Have you gotten any closer to him?"

I shouldn't tell him the truth; I knew the havoc it would wreak upon his psyche. He was an intelligence specialist to the core, responsible for informing the actions of the trigger-pullers he guided along the precipice of their service to the Handler. One miscalculation on his part meant their freefall to certain death, and all but he and I had already paid that price. They had all failed to spot the worst threat possible: the one that resided in the chair next to them, undetected.

But the truth about that failure could be the knockout blow that kept Ian from dying in a fight he couldn't win.

I tossed the bait. "I've gotten close enough to kill him."

"Matz?"

"Caspian."

For the first time, Ian's pallor indicated the same fear that I felt. His mouth hung open for a second, and then he began muttering quietly, almost to himself, "We had good intel that Caspian was killed. Good intel. There will be consequences to how the team reacted, and now we need to move against the Handler quicker than I thought."

"Look, the Handler's people knew I was coming. Don't trust this inside source."

"And instead rely on—what, exactly? You think I've got a grab bag of other options besides my source and you? If you don't get this done, then I'm the last man standing. It'll be up to me."

"No, it won't. You can still walk away."

His eyes narrowed and he forced his gaze forward, out the window. When he spoke again, his voice was more resolute than I'd ever heard him. "You're forgetting that I was in that vehicle with Karma when she was shot. I'd known her, and Boss's whole team, for years before you ever showed up. And since I failed to detect that Caspian faked his death, then I'm responsible for letting the team die. So I will get revenge against the Handler, David. With or without you."

In trying to deter him, I'd thrown water on a grease fire.

"Ian, just—"

"Tell me how to find him."

I sighed mightily, knowing full well that he'd self-destruct in his quest if I didn't beat him to killing the Handler. But I also knew I was going to die upon my return from the mission, and if I didn't tell Ian what little information I'd gathered, revenge for Karma would likely never happen. And any deep cover agent would be seeking corroboration for my details about the Silver Widow, the one facet of the Somalia mission that the Handler had been concerned with.

Ian only wanted to know how to find his enemy.

"You're looking for a jet," I said. "It landed at the Complex somewhere outside San Antonio yesterday. 10:30 local time. No tail number. Return takeoff within ten minutes. Flight time estimated at four hours, temperature at the destination was around freezing. We launched again last night. Best guess, it was a two-hour flight to SEATAC. They moved me blind so I'm not sure if they put a tail number on."

"What else?"

"He's got an electric chair. That's how he killed the Indian. That's why my head is shaved. Now I'm about to go on a mission I don't understand for a reason I don't know, and between Caspian's betrayal and what the Handler must know already, this goes deeper than we realize. That's why the more I see, the less I want you involved in this."

"I can't sleep anymore." His voice sounded frail, vulnerable. "And if you can't see this through to the end, then I will."

My vision blurred amid the white void of sky outside the window. "Be careful, Ian."

I pushed myself to my feet.

"It was nice meeting you," I said, loudly enough for any immediate bystanders to hear.

Then I walked away before he could object, leaving my glass where it rested.

3

January 3, 2009
Galeão International Airport
Rio de Janeiro, Brazil

I exited the baggage claim to a wave of morning air satu-
rated with humidity and vehicle exhaust—already too hot
for the suit I wore. The sidewalks were lined with people,
mostly locals waiting for families. A few tourists were
among them, departing in yellow compact cars whose
spot on the curb was quickly filled by overzealous taxi
drivers searching for their next fare.

Walking down the sidewalk, I spotted the silver sedan
parked amid a row of taxis. Its trunk popped open as I
approached, and I leaned down to see the driver through
the open passenger window. He had "Complex operator"
written all over him: loose shirt selected for concealing
the pistol on his waist and the full-sleeve tattoos on his

arms, broad face and shoulders indicating a few years of steroid use that had more than repaid the investment.

But when he spoke it was in a boyish voice, a near-lisp at the end of my name. "Your chariot awaits, Mr. Rivers."

I tossed my luggage in the trunk and let myself in. "They sent a supermodel to pick me up from the Complex. You're something of a letdown."

He raised an eyebrow. "That blonde who runs the budget?"

"Redhead."

"Meh. Not my style." He pulled away from the curb and gunned the car forward, adding a wary, "Sir."

"David."

"Right on. I'm Reilly. Your kit's in the glove compartment."

I opened it to find a Glock 19 inside a concealable holster with belt clips, two spare magazines, cell phone, sports watch, and a money clip stuffed with a thick roll of Brazilian currency. A quick check revealed the pistol to be loaded and chambered with hollow points.

I looked at him, failing to mask my annoyance. "This it?"

"Yeah."

"Really?"

"Yeah."

I slid the full holster inside my waistband, arranging my suit jacket over it before pocketing the spare magazines.

"What does the watch do, shoot a laser?"

"Tracking device with ninety-six hours of beacon transmit. Same as the money clip."

I put it on my wrist, then pocketed the phone and waved the money clip at Reilly.

"I guess I can use this to buy some fucking body armor and a radio earpiece. Where the hell is the rest of my kit? How am I supposed to communicate with the security detail?"

"I'm just a medic, bro. Everyone else is on duty, and that's all they gave me for the handoff. You were a last-minute addition to the team."

"Then I hope you know about the mission, because no one prior to this point has filled me in."

"Standard business negotiation. Our delegation has one primary, two staffers, a translator, and eight bodyguards. Meeting location is unknown, host organization is providing transportation."

"How are the beacons monitored?"

"Fixed-wing ISR bird up top." A stab of fear shot through me—instantly, irrationally, I was back on the hilltop seeing Caspian's bloodied face as he looked up to scan the sky.

He's probably watching right now...

I shook the thought clear, blinking myself back to reality as Reilly continued casually, "...week's worth of airspace clearance for aerial tourism charters, and weather looks good. Shouldn't be any gaps in coverage."

If the sky at present was any indication, he was right. Drenched in shifting cobalt hues, the rising sun's light was arrested only by a few smears of cloud that wouldn't inhibit aerial observation for long.

But on someone else's turf, even small gaps could make all the difference.

"What about ground team?"

He swerved our car around a maintenance van with its emergency flashers on. "Usual crew from tech branch tracking on foot and cars running parallels to triangulate the beacons. Eight Outfit shooters trailing the delegation in vehicles just in case shit hits the fan. And it's hard to see, but can you spot the boat with the chopper out there?"

He was peering out the driver's side window, stabbing a finger at the glass. I looked past a blur of traffic flowing the opposite direction as the road arced onto a bridge over the water. Among smaller ships in the calm waters of the bay, I saw a distant freighter lurking. A helicopter was visible on the open deck between clusters of stacked shipping containers.

"I see it. How big is the quick reaction force?"

"Twelve Outfit shooters stationed on the boat with the flight crew. And me, until I had to come get you. Best thing to happen to me all trip. We've been sucking dick for gas money out there, living in shipping containers, and playing soccer on the deck in between no-notice rehearsal launches for three days now. But when the call comes, we're off like a prom dress. Ten-minute flight time to South Zone, where the delegation is staying." He glanced over at me, weighing his next words with a measured casualness. "You just came back from that Somalia mission?"

I looked at him, trying to gauge his intent and seeing only a nervous curiosity. If this was a deliberate test to see if I'd bend the rules of confidentiality, it wasn't a good one.

"I'm not supposed to talk about that."

"And I'm not supposed to ask. But here we are." He was still watching me, only glancing at the lane ahead as an afterthought, waiting for a response.

"How do I know you're not going to rat me out?"

"Cut the shit, bro. Before the Outfit, what were you? MARSOC? You're not tan enough to be a SEAL."

"Ranger."

"Well *Sua Sponte*, motherfucker. I spent five years as a Ranger medic. That's what I'm talking about, see? We all go to war together before the Outfit, and now some criminals who've never gone to combat tell us not to talk to each other while we go die for their operation. I heard you came back from Somalia alone."

"I did."

He winced. "Your partner was a good fucker, man. Helped me out a lot when I got to the Outfit."

"How do you know who my partner was?"

"Saw you guys heading to the airfield for some practice freefalls at the Complex before I had to ship down here with the advance team. Did his body make it back home?"

"Yeah."

"You sure?"

"I carried him off the plane."

"Good. He deserves to be buried at the Complex. How was the memorial?"

"They sent me here before it happened. Now shoot it to me straight. What's the rumor mill saying about this mission?"

"Usual shit. The organization down here has already set the cheapest terms they'll agree to, and the Handler's spies figured them out already. It's going to be a one-day handshake deal."

"So what am I supposed to do?"

He gave an exaggerated laugh, looking at me as if I'd lost my mind. "If I were you? Be glad you got promoted out of the Complex. You'll be getting paid a lot more, and your odds of getting shot in the face just went down by a factor of ten."

"What about the fact no one knows where the meeting will take place?"

"This is my sixth delegation security op in six countries. Only one of those involved knowing the meeting location ahead of time. All of them were the easiest paycheck I've ever made."

We came alongside a blue-and-silver commuter bus, and I watched the row of faces within as we cruised past. Glancing back to Reilly, I asked, "Then why is the Handler staging so many shooters in Rio?"

"Break glass in case of emergency, my friend. The Outfit's not going to see any action here, much less you. Even if things went sideways, you think the delegation's bodyguards are going to let you take over? The only reason you're here is because the boss said so."

"Brazil's got one of the highest murder rates in the world."

"Sure, in the favelas. You think a multi-million-dollar deal is being made in some shantytown in the hills run by drug traffickers? The delegation is waiting for you at a beach with the most expensive real estate on the continent."

"Then why did the Handler personally order me here?"

He fell silent abruptly, his eyes steeling to the road. I looked ahead, expecting a crash, but our lane was clear. An industrial district swept by to my right, the silos dotting a horizon that revealed glimpses of mountains in the distance. It was far from the tourist image of Rio I'd been expecting.

"'Personally' ordered you?" Reilly asked, tentative. "You mean, you met him?"

"To say the least."

"Like, they flew you to the Mist Palace?"

"I guess. Where is it?"

"You're the one who went."

"I couldn't see out the plane's windows, and you're the one who's been in the Outfit longer than a month. Where is it?"

"I'm supposed to report you for asking."

"And I'm supposed to report myself for telling you I went. Your head isn't on the chopping block when you get back from this, but mine is. *Sua Sponte*, motherfucker."

Reilly hesitated before answering.

"I mean, I've heard it's somewhere in Washington." He cleared his throat. "Maybe across the border in Canada."

"What else?"

"That's it. The only people who know the exact location are the pilots who need to find the airstrip."

He looked at me uncomfortably. I realized I had shifted in my seat, completely focused on him as I awaited more information.

"All right." I swiftly changed the subject. "Tell me about the primary for the Handler's delegation. Who is he?"

Reilly shot me a quizzical glance. "They really didn't tell you shit, did they? The primary on this one isn't a he. It's a *she*."

* * *

The tunnel through which we traveled was a mirror of my thoughts—channelized, dimly lit, and flying toward a single destination that glowed luminous in the distance. Had my warning to Ian reduced his drive to hunt the Handler? Probably not. Given his words and the sheer audacity required to approach me in the airport in the first place, only the Handler's death would stop him. Ian and I sought the same thing, and while my death was certain, Ian still had a chance of living beyond our dark obsession and emerging with some semblance of a normal life.

Our car exited the tunnel. Blazing sunlight revealed the crystalline expanse of a vast lake and, beyond it, my first up-close glimpse of the arcing, jungled hills of Rio's tourist ideal. It was a vision of unspeakable beauty that contrasted with the darkness of the tunnel, but Reilly began humming a tune before I could enjoy the view.

I looked at him. He raised his eyebrows suggestively, then began humming louder. It sounded like elevator music.

"You okay?" I asked.

"We're driving into Ipanema."

"So?"

"As in 'The Girl from Ipanema?' Sinatra?"

I shrugged.

He shook his head sadly at my ignorance. "World-class neighborhood, and we're just passing through on our way to Leblon. Even more upscale there. You think this view is good, you've got no idea what's coming up."

The road turned south and away from the lake and we cruised into urban sprawl. The geography was suddenly muted by the imprint of man, an ecosystem that could have been any number of cities in America's humid, subtropical regions.

"Check it out—this is where you'll be working, you lucky bastard."

A right turn swung us broadside to the gleaming surface of the South Atlantic, the sapphire water separated from us by a few lanes of opposing traffic and a beach dotted with sunbathers.

"You've never seen bikinis like this in the States," Reilly continued. "Something you may not know about me, David—I'm nothing if not an ass man."

"I was just about to ask."

"Riding out this trip on the freighter while this kind of talent parades around the beaches from sunup to sundown makes me sick to my stomach."

I gave him a sideways look. "There a point to this line of conversation, Reilly?"

"Not really."

I grinned at his childish voice applied to the women of Rio. The casual sunbathers were dispersed along the coast, far outnumbered by people walking and riding bicycles along a path beside the road. The lanes were split by a narrow median of perfectly spaced palm trees reminiscent of Beverly Hills.

He pulled our car into a hotel inlet, stopping before the glass lobby doors.

"Here we are," he said wistfully. "Le Chateaux Mer. Have fun living my dream."

"Hope your dream's a good one, brother. Thanks for the lift."

A valet stepped forward to open my door as Reilly popped the trunk from the driver's seat and began barking orders in crude Brazilian Portuguese.

I stepped out as the valet hurried to the trunk to retrieve my luggage and a tall, middle-aged man dressed in an unbuttoned tan suit approached us gracefully from the hotel doors. He bent forward slightly at the waist and gave Reilly a single nod through the car window.

After the valet slammed the trunk, Reilly pulled forward and turned right onto the street.

"Mr. Rivers?" the well-dressed man said. He was in his late forties, thinning auburn hair neatly combed. If Reilly had been easily identifiable as an Outfit operator, then the man before me was equally discernable as a bodyguard; like Reilly, he appeared a shooter at heart, though his appearance was enameled by years of close proximity to an elite class who warranted protection but were unable to provide it for themselves.

"David," I responded.

He handed a sky-blue bill to the valet, and my luggage was whisked inside.

"Micah. Security lead. Your role," he said in a low voice, "is to be a wallflower in this delegation. Go where my people tell you to go, sit where they tell you to sit. The first time anyone but me hears your voice will be when you say goodbye upon our return."

Forcing a smile, I said, "You must have me confused with someone who asked to be here."

"We follow the orders we're given. But do not underestimate the consequences of failing to stay out of my staff's way."

Before I could answer, a group of people exited the hotel and stood beneath the overhang. Close to a dozen individuals made up the entourage, mostly men and all dressed for business. Half wore the same unbuttoned suit jacket as Micah, paired with the subdued vigilance of a private security detail.

The cast of players surrounded a single young woman. She was their center of orbit, and a strange one at that— not by virtue of her gender, for there were other women, but by her youth. I doubted she was over thirty. Unlike the others in her party, she carried herself with the somber petulance of one bearing a responsibility outweighing everyone else's. Brunette hair so dark it appeared nearly black fell unadorned to her collarbone. Her face appeared free of cosmetics other than dark eye shadow and eyeliner, and her broad range of jewelry looked like an afterthought added by a painter's final strokes that crossed the line into excess.

I felt an unsettling burning sensation in my stomach, though whether discomfort or desire, I couldn't tell. Who the fuck was this woman?

The girl from Ipanema, I thought.

Her body, a half-step removed from gangly, was lean beneath her business attire. She watched the screen of a phone being proffered by an aide beside her, then suddenly looked up at me. We locked eyes for a second, her electric green irises shocking against her heart-shaped face.

In that moment, the woman looked like a child cast out to sea, vulnerable and alone amid an ocean that she had no control over.

Micah stepped in front of my gaze, blocking my view of the woman. "Make no mistake: I report directly to the One. If you fail to tread lightly, there will be repercussions."

I faced Micah, feeling the tingling mix of irritation and rage bubbling inside me, an all-too-familiar sensation that generally preceded my saying something I shouldn't.

"As much as I enjoy getting threatened," I said, leveling my eyes at him, "I already heard this number from your puppet master. He delivered it better. So how about keeping an eye on your primary instead of wasting your attention on an expendable extra."

His face intensified with anger, and as he opened his mouth to speak, the woman appeared beside us.

"David, welcome to Brazil," she said. Her voice was outwardly courteous, but I detected an undertow of inconvenience—she wasn't any happier about my presence than Micah. "Thank you for making the journey."

I said nothing. Why was I supposed to protect this woman?

She wasn't traditionally beautiful, I told myself—her face was very much representative of the plain and innocuous supporting actress role at the casting agency. Strong, thick, sculpted eyebrows, chin a bit too prominent. Tall; lanky even. Not my style.

Her smoky eyes took in my shaved head and softened, watching me with an expectant stare. I opened my mouth in the same manner that had many times allowed a rapier wit to take the lead before my mind could deliberately form a thought.

No sound came forth, and instead I sealed my lips and nodded.

She turned to Micah. "Make sure David understands—"

"I've already spoken to him, Ms. Parvaneh."

The impasse between Micah, Parvaneh, and myself was arrested by the appearance of a black Chevrolet Suburban at the hotel entrance.

It rumbled in slowly, its surfaces waxed to a mirror shine. I grasped its significance at once by the delegation's reaction. All talking ceased, and all eyes turned to the SUV. It came to a halt, its body reflecting our images back at us. When the engine went silent, I realized how loud it had been—the echo faded like a receding thunderbolt. No ordinary V-8 under the hood.

The driver exited the truck and approached us.

He walked briskly for his immense size, a radio earpiece visible as he removed his sunglasses. I could see the bulk of a shoulder holster beneath his left armpit.

Parvaneh greeted him warmly. "*Bom dia, senhor.* How may I help you?"

He stopped before her, responding in thickly accented English, "Good morning, ma'am. I am here to take you to the meeting."

Micah said, "Where are the rest of your vehicles?"

"I am afraid it is just me. Recent security concerns have forced us to take additional precautions, and the delay of this meeting has exacerbated these concerns considerably."

Parvaneh said, "How many people may we take?"

"I have four open seats—"

"Four?" Micah hotly interceded. "We were assured transportation for a delegation of thirteen. This is a breach of our terms."

"I am afraid my employer has set these conditions, not me. You are free to leave if they are not satisfactory. But this is perfectly safe." He tapped his radio earpiece. "The meeting location has even been safeguarded from me—I will receive directions as we proceed. Your vehicle is armored against high-powered rifle rounds. Bomb blankets, run-flat tires. See for yourself."

He turned to the Suburban, straining to swing open the heavy back door.

In a split second, I was wracked with horror.

The SUV's interior was a blood-splattered wasteland. In the far seat was Karma's motionless body, slumped forward. Her face was a savage void of gore.

"See?" the driver said. "Perfectly safe."

I grabbed Parvaneh's wrist and was met at once by Micah's steel grip on my forearm.

"Don't get in," I said, my eyes locked on the interior.

The driver looked at me, unsure if I was a decision maker and not seeming too concerned either way. "You are free to decline, of course. Perhaps the meeting can be rescheduled for a later date."

She slowly pulled her wrist free from my hand, her eyes moving to Micah's rather than mine.

He shook his head subtly.

Parvaneh's eyes were flat, heavy with the veiled magnitude of the decision she was about to make, for better or worse. I felt my stomach churn with dread—the situation couldn't have been any more clear-cut to Micah and me, but we weren't calling the shots.

Without another second's hesitation, Parvaneh said, "We agree to his terms."

Micah lifted his hand from my arm.

The driver replied, "Very well. We may depart whenever you are ready." He left the back door ajar and returned to his seat behind the wheel.

Micah cleared his throat and whispered, "Ma'am, I must strongly advise you to—"

She silenced him with a subtle turn of her hand, palm down in a horizontal slice. Then she lifted the same hand to gently rest her fingertips on his shoulder. "We're going. I'll need you with me."

His response was immediate. "I hear and I obey."

Turning to the waiting group behind her, she said, "Gabriel."

A slight whisper of a man stepped forward. He was dark-skinned, with a pointed nose and dark eyes that shifted nervously. But his voice was perfectly steady as he spoke in the native accent. "I hear and I obey, ma'am."

Her stare swept over the delegation before settling on me with a subtle hint of inner conflict. The Handler had ordered me to stay by her side, and Parvaneh had no authority to disregard this command no matter the circumstances. I knew what she was going to say before she spoke.

"And you, David."

Then she turned away from me, reaching for the passenger door. Micah stopped her with a soft touch and whispered, "I need you to sit in the back, middle seat."

"I ride in the front," she said coolly.

"Ma'am, I implore you."

A pause before she nodded her consent. She slipped in the back as Micah turned to me with a pained expression, his voice hushed. "I want you behind the driver."

I looked at him. "Bullshit aside—if this goes badly, you can count on me."

He didn't reply, turning instead to enter the passenger seat as I rounded the vehicle. I pulled open the heavy back door, watching the empty space where I'd seen Karma's body a moment before. Parvaneh was staring at me strangely now, sensing my weakness and not appreciating the view. Gabriel slid into the open seat opposite me, uneasily fastening his seatbelt.

My blood curdled as I entered the vehicle, my breath quickening with my betrayal of all instinct.

The heavy, armored doors of the Suburban slammed shut like gunshots. The driver pulled forward to the street, accelerating away from the remaining members of the delegation who stood with blank expressions, watching our departure in silence.

* * *

An increasingly complex series of quick turns led us away
from the hotel as the driver responded to instructions over
his radio earpiece. I watched the surrounding traffic, scanning civilian vehicles, taxis, and commuter buses and idly
wondering which belonged to the surveillance team
following us. I found no evidence to justify the fear that
consumed me with each passing second, and yet I felt like
an animal snared, waiting for the arrival of an unhurried
trapper.

Every turn revealed a street as affluent as the last. I
had been conditioned by military deployments to watch
for the suddenly empty urban setting, the absence of children that preceded many an ambush where the locals
either sensed or implicitly knew that bullets would soon
start flying. But the sidewalks were host to a wide array of
men and women strolling or waiting at crosswalks, the
storefronts passing by much as a journey through any
peaceful city.

We reached the giant lake I'd first seen with Reilly,
skirting its southern border until we cut into a city street
that descended toward an oceanfront road. The beach was
dotted with umbrellas and volleyball nets, swimmers and
sunbathers in abundance as we proceeded northeast
along the coast.

Nonetheless, I had the implacable sense of imminent
disaster lurking ahead. Judging by Parvaneh's wardrobe,
she didn't have a weapon; while I couldn't tell whether
Gabriel did or not, the anxious jumpiness of his nervous
eyes made me confident that he would be dead weight or
worse in the event of a crisis. His face was made up of
exaggerated features—long nose, fleshy lips—and the flat-

tering cut of his suit couldn't compensate for the scrawniness of the body beneath. Whatever his role in the Organization, he wasn't a fighter.

Micah's poise, by contrast, was the only comfort to be had.

He was alert as a falcon in the passenger seat, his head pivoting with smooth precision, the movement stuttering and reversing when something new caught his eye. I knew for a fact he was armed, and while I was unsure of his experience, he hadn't been hired as Parvaneh's security lead because he was bad at his job.

Reaching into my pocket, I felt for my tracking device disguised as a money clip. Separating the folded bills, I pulled out the clip and shoved it deep into the crevice of the seat between my thigh and Parvaneh's. As my hand brushed her leg, she flexed her left hand into a fist that bore an engagement ring and wedding band. The latter was crowned with an enormous princess-cut diamond, the same cut—though probably three times the size—of the one that I'd bought for my fiancée before our engagement had imploded two years ago.

The Suburban turned left between high-rise buildings, coming to a stop behind a row of cars parked at a sidewalk inlet. The driver said, "Here we are."

Micah said, "Gabriel?"

"Copacabana," Gabriel replied. "This is a safe area."

We exited amid a row of office buildings to find a politely smiling, fair-skinned Brazilian woman wearing a form-fitting knee-length skirt. As she invited us inside, I appraised our surroundings but couldn't find the slightest threat: we were in the middle of a city block like the rest we had passed, the building before us appearing in every way to be an ordinary structure.

Micah took the lead, walking ahead with Parvaneh as I waited for Gabriel to pass me. We entered a lobby with clean, modern decor, the smooth, white-tiled surfaces extending down a hallway as our hostess led us past open double doors and into a conference room.

Inside was a long table with a man standing on either side, their hands empty.

Parvaneh asked, "Where is my counterpart, *senhora*?"

Our hostess smiled. "I apologize for the inconvenience, but at this point we must insist that any items transmitting your location to outside parties be removed from your persons, including cell phones. This is to ensure the safety of our employer, who, as you know, prefers discretion. Once he has left the meeting location, your items will be returned to you."

Score one for the money clip I'd hidden in the Suburban, I thought. Parvaneh nodded her permission to us, removing first her phone and then her bracelet and setting them on the table.

Gabriel slid a wedding ring from his finger and set his phone beside it, and Micah tossed down his phone and a pocketknife. I surrendered the phone I'd been given, leaving my watch with the tracking device on my wrist as I stepped back with the others.

Then our hostess said, "I am afraid you must leave your weapons as well."

Micah replied, "Your employer must understand that asking a visiting delegation to surrender them before arrival to the meeting site is no sign of trust."

"Be that as it may, sir, we have our orders. You are free to cancel the negotiations and we will return you to your party at Le Chateaux Mer at once."

Parvaneh cut a glance toward Micah and said, "We are happy to honor the stipulations of our gracious host."

Micah and I removed our pistol holsters and set them down, followed by the extra magazines.

Our hostess bowed her head in gratitude. "All that remains is a brief scan before you proceed to the meeting."

At this, one of the men beside the table stepped forward and procured a foot-long handheld wand from his belt, then scanned it over my body. It whirred to life with a garbled, high-pitched whine as it passed over my wrist.

The man stepped back as our hostess said, "The watch, please."

I took it off my wrist and tossed it on the table, then received another full sweep before the man moved on to Micah.

Micah did worse than me—he lost his belt and an innocuous-looking hotel key card. Gabriel fared the same, giving up a wallet and a business card holder. But Parvaneh took the prize, her face holding a composed air of dignity each time the detector howled.

"Your earrings, please."

"And your necklace, ma'am."

"Your pen."

"Your rings."

By the time she passed the inspection, virtually every item she possessed had been surrendered. Even the giant glittering wedding ring was gone now, though the engagement band remained. The second man placed the confiscated items into separate zippered vinyl pouches and then put all four in a single backpack that he handed to our hostess.

With that, we were escorted back to the waiting Suburban. Our hostess took the lead, carrying the backpack with our confiscated items.

As we trailed her, Micah strode alongside me and whispered, "They're about to throw our surveillance. The driver's packing a shoulder holster."

"I noticed."

"If I go down, get his gun."

"If you go down, I'll enjoy some peace and quiet."

As we returned to our previous seats, our hostess handed the backpack to the driver, who unzipped it and plucked my hidden money clip from a cup holder beside him. He held it up so those of us in the back could see, and then deposited it inside the backpack.

"Must have fallen out of my pocket," I suggested blithely. Parvaneh looked at me, incensed.

Our driver said nothing, pulling back into traffic.

The presence of our confiscated tracking devices within the vehicle amounted to a public service announcement that we were about to lose our aerial surveillance, just as Micah had said. As long as the ground team was able to maintain sight of us, I reminded myself, we still had some semblance of protection if we were headed into an ambush.

Our driver spun a wild U-turn at an intersection, speeding three blocks back the way we'd come before making a hard turn into an underground parking garage. After he accelerated forward and around a curve, tires screeching, I saw a second black Suburban identical to ours.

Braking to a sharp halt beside the doppelganger truck, our driver opened his door and handed off the bag containing our trackers to a man leaning out of the opposite vehicle. The other Suburban then raced forward and out of the garage to be reacquired by our aircraft and surveillance teams. Our driver reversed into a parking spot and pulled back out in the opposite direction, cutting left to exit onto a separate street.

I wanted to fight the driver at this point, but the rest of my party remained silent throughout the exchange. Was this normal for them? Parvaneh's face was stoic, and I couldn't read Micah's expression. Gabriel gazed out the window the entire time, though whether he was in a daze or ticking off familiar landmarks, I had no idea.

As we rolled past a stoplight and onto another street, I looked about for any sign of surveillance. There was no way to tell if the handoff had succeeded in confusing our watchers. Regardless, our situation was rapidly deteriorating beyond the ability of any security measures to save us—reduced from a full delegation to four unarmed individuals likely untracked by any protective forces employed by the Handler.

We cruised into a short tunnel cutting into a foothill. The far-right lane was blocked by another black Suburban, its four-way flashers blinking rhythmically against the arcing tunnel roof. We pulled up behind it, and our driver activated his flashers as the other truck accelerated forward into traffic.

"North into Botafogo?" Micah asked.

"Correct," Gabriel replied. "This is a popular tourist area. No problem."

After a half-minute of cars whooshing past to our left, the driver pulled forward and we passed into the waning sunlight of a major city center.

Two turns off the main road took us into a private parking garage with a manned guard station, the striped barrier rising automatically as we approached. I tilted my head to see a small white access device clipped to the driver's folded sun visor—at this point, anyone left from the surveillance team would have to follow us on foot, and the security guard wasn't about to let that happen.

The driver guided our truck down a spiraling path to the third sublevel before speeding forward to an elevator, where a bearded man waited.

The Suburban came to a stop and our driver said, "You are to enter the elevator, please."

As soon as we stepped out of the vehicle, the driver pulled forward and headed for the exit, surely to continue distracting any remaining surveillance assets.

The bearded man greeted us formally, gesturing to the elevator.

"Ms. Parvaneh, gentlemen, thank you for coming and welcome to Rio de Janeiro. If you care to come with me, the meeting will begin shortly."

* * *

He was well-built, with a dense beard that stood in contrast to his attire—slacks with a razor crease, dress shirt pulled tight across his flat stomach. No place to conceal a weapon, and no wardrobe for someone who intended to cause harm.

"*Obrigado*," Parvaneh said, "for receiving our party."

"Madam, it is no trouble at all. First let me apologize for the security measures— in the past days there has been greater intelligence reporting than is normal. My employer has taken additional precautions in order to attend the meeting as planned."

The elevator doors closed behind us with a pleasant chime as the interior lights glowed to life.

We began our journey upward as Parvaneh replied, "Of course we understand. Your employer's intimate knowledge of this land is what brings us here to discuss a closer alliance, *senhor*."

The two continued exchanging polite banalities until our elevator halted at the top floor. We disembarked to a private suite with wraparound windows.

The protective security detail was visible immediately —eight men arrayed across the suite, short hair, earpieces, and vigilant gazes matched by Micah as he took three steps into the suite and scanned the scene.

So too was the protected party apparent at once. Advancing to meet us were two men and a woman led by a rotund Latino man easily in his sixties. His smile was fixed below glasses, his watery eyes magnified by thick lenses.

"*Bem-vinda, senhora!*" he exclaimed, extending his hand to Parvaneh.

She accepted his handshake, her diplomatic response muffled as he pulled her close to kiss both of her cheeks.

As he released her, she managed to say, "*Obrigada, Senhor* Ribeiro. We are honored to represent our organization in your presence..." As she spoke, Gabriel began chattering in Portuguese.

Ribeiro's eyes remained fixed on Parvaneh's, but he nodded in cadence to Gabriel's translation.

When Ribeiro responded, Gabriel translated, "First, let us eat together as friends. Then we may speak as businesspeople. We have had some of the finest chefs in Rio prepare dinner for your party."

Our collective group was ushered forward to a set of

double doors, beyond which was a wide table beautifully arrayed with vases of flowers and exquisite banquet plates of food, the place settings lining the table before high-backed chairs. An extravagant crystal chandelier guarded the preparations, sparkling with dazzling rays of light and color.

As the group filtered in, Micah placed a hand on my arm and said, "Wait out here."

I stopped in place and one of the guards closed the double doors behind the party, separating the insiders from the outsiders, literally and symbolically. The guard turned to me and gave a curt nod to his side, where I saw a buffet table holding steel food pans of the continental breakfast variety.

Scraps for the commoners, I thought. I took a step toward it, but my advance was barred by half the body-guards descending on the food, piling their plates high and moving to a scattered arrangement of coffee tables and lounge chairs. The rest paced throughout the suite, remaining on duty as they waited their turn at the conso-lation table.

In the next hour I ate two plates of food alone, the body-guards murmuring among themselves as if I weren't there. After I couldn't stomach any more fried plantains, I deposited my plate in a stack with the others and strolled to the window.

From the penthouse vantage point, I looked upon the early evening view of Rio de Janeiro, the city a glistening gem nestled between sapphire sea and emerald moun-tains. Structure gave way to jungle when the elevation became too steep to build on, the alternating mishmash of man and nature descending until it vanished altogether into the Atlantic.

I thought of grabbing Parvaneh's wrist and telling her not to get in the truck. After Afghanistan and Iraq, after my time with Boss's team and Caspian in Somalia, had my constant exposure to danger finally gotten the best of me? Perhaps I'd been pushed to the edge of near-death circumstances one too many times. Considering what I'd seen, my judgment could have understandably been warped into a flawed paranoia.

My mind resisted this dismissal: I had seen Karma's dead body in the seat of the Suburban, just as surely as I'd seen it the moments after her death.

Then I remembered what Caspian told me. *Survivor's guilt is a motherfucker, David. And there's no outliving that.*

"Do you see our Redeemer?" a voice beside me asked.

I turned to see the bearded man from the elevator looking intently out the window.

"Excuse me?"

He pointed to a perilously steep rock face rising to a craggy summit overlooking the kingdom below. At its peak was the whitewashed figure of Christ with arms extended, an iconic symbol of Rio that I recognized even at a distance.

"We call him *Cristo Redentor*. Christ the Redeemer. He has watched over Rio for seventy-seven years. Last year he was struck by lightning, but still he stands."

"I wish I were so resilient."

"Yes. Yes, as do I. What is your name, my friend?"

"David."

"I am Agustin. You seem to have injured yourself."

Turning to him with a quizzical glance, I realized he

was looking at the welt on my shorn scalp. I'd almost forgotten it was there, though the event was clear enough in my memory: Racegun bringing the leather sap over my skull before I was strapped to the electric chair.

"I fell down some stairs," I said flatly.

"I also noticed you were not allowed into the meeting, which makes me wonder why you were brought here in the first place."

"That's an excellent question."

"This is life, no? You work as diligently as you can, you try to earn the trust of those above you, and sometimes the door closes nonetheless."

"I suppose so."

His brow was furrowed, chocolate eyes intense with thought. "And here we are, you and I, cast out by the masters. But I tell you, we are the lucky ones. The room in which our employers toil over profits and numbers, over kilos and grams, does not have a window. Here we are, sharing this view in the moment, the only time we have."

He took a contemplative step back from the window, then reversed the movement to scrutinize the landscape once more. "You have not yet told me what you thought of our Redeemer."

I raised my eyes upward to Christ's figure on the hill. "It's magnificent. Truly. Your whole city is...beautiful. Truly beautiful."

He released a quick breath, his eyes fixed on the distant statue. "I am not from Brazil originally. I came here when I was eight years old, without money, without a family. On that first night, terrified, I saw him on that mountain, glowing white and watching over me. And I knew at that moment that I was home. He has guided my life ever since, and I have been more fortunate than I ever dreamed of. Are you a man of faith?"

I shook my head slightly.

He said, "Perhaps one day."

"Perhaps." I pointed out the window. "What about the space between the city and mountain?"

He glanced at a craggy line of irregular salmon-colored roofs crawling uphill, dividing lush jungle from civilized urban sprawl. The ramshackle buildings looked unspeakably grotesque next to the clean beige structures of Rio, like trash accumulated in the corners of an otherwise spotless civilization.

"Santa Marta." He nodded. "One of our many favelas. The result of soldiers and slaves who could afford to live nowhere else, and a problem my government has never remedied. Many think of them as dangerous places. And it is true—violent drug traffickers live within, desperate young men high on their product who battle over territory. Much senseless death. But that is not the truth of the favelas."

"What is?"

"Aside from this criminal minority, the residents of the hills are humble, hardworking people. For over a century they have thrived without any government assistance—indeed, even the buildings themselves are built upon solid rock. If you lived among them for a time, you would see a culture, resourcefulness, and resilience unmatched by the grandest privilege of Rio. They have bonded in life more than most ever will with their neighbor. This makes them family, so they have everything. You understand this bond, yes?"

I thought of those I'd bonded with in life—my ex-fiancée and the best friend she had an affair with. Then

Remy from the Army, my BASE jumping mentor Jackson, Boss, Matz, Ophie, Karma, Caspian—all dead.

"Of course."

"Then you have all the family you need, and more. A man who lacks that is very poor indeed, no matter the success he achieves elsewhere in life. Tell me—"

His phone chimed in his pocket, and he looked at it quickly with a mournful grimace. "Ah, the meeting draws to a close. I must see that your vehicle is prepared to return you to Le Chateaux Mer. These security precautions are...tedious. But necessary. If I may offer you one piece of advice?"

"Please."

"Remember that Rio de Janeiro is like life, David." He touched my arm, and I was surprised not to find myself angered by the gesture as he nodded out the window. "If you ever get lost, you can always look to Christ to find the way."

"Indeed. It was a pleasure meeting you, Agustin."

"I feel the same. And I must tell you"—he lowered his voice—"it is unlikely we shall ever meet again. But if we do, know that you may call on me for anything. Anything at all."

"Perhaps one day it will be us behind closed doors together."

He smiled at the thought, but then his expression sobered as he nodded solemnly. "Perhaps one day."

We shook hands for the first time. His grip was brief but powerful, matched by a respectful bow of his head before he released my hand and disappeared within the elevator.

Upon his departure, the bodyguards in the suite lapsed into silence and stood, virtually in unison. They swiftly assumed their places in the array that had met us upon our arrival to the suite, a cast of characters taking their places on a stage that they didn't question.

The double doors of the conference room swung open as Ribeiro and Parvaneh led the procession back into the suite. They were conversing easily now, their words exchanged as if Gabriel weren't translating between them, traversing effortlessly from Portuguese to English and back again.

I waited on the periphery of the exalted class as they swept toward the elevators, Ribeiro boarding one with four of his bodyguards while the other three members of his party entered the second.

The light above each set of doors indicated that both elevators were headed up, not down.

A bodyguard stepped before us and said, "*Um minuto, por favor.*"

"Why?" Micah asked.

Looking irritated, the bodyguard spoke quickly to Gabriel.

Gabriel nodded and translated, "He says we must wait until his people have departed."

He hadn't yet finished his sentence when I heard the steady drum of rotor blades. Looking to the window, I saw a white helicopter approaching from the early evening sky, lit by a red and green light on either side of its fuselage as it crested the roof overhead. We heard the thundering hum of it touching down above us, muting the suite to a hushed silence for a full minute as conversation became impractical over the vibration of churning rotor blades. The noise lifted suddenly as the helicopter took off in a different direction, remaining absent from our view inside the suite.

The bodyguard's head ticked sideways for a moment before he raised a finger to his earpiece and said into his cuff, "*Afirmativo.*" Then he pressed the down button, and the steel doors slid apart to reveal an empty elevator.

He looked to us with a brightened expression. "*Entrem, por favor.*"

We stepped into the elevator and he entered behind us, illuminating the third parking garage sublevel button with a touch of his finger.

The doors slid shut, and we began our descent.

The bodyguard led the way into the parking garage, signaling us to wait as we left the elevator.

We stopped in place as he proceeded toward the idling black Suburban, the window lowered eight inches to partially expose our driver's face. Given that it was an armored vehicle, I thought, that was probably as far as the ballistic glass window would descend.

As the bodyguard leaned against the door to exchange words with the driver, Parvaneh spoke quietly to Micah.

"Speak the truth."

With a lowered voice, he said, "I've been accompanying delegations since you were only a child. And that was the most gracefully handled negotiation I've seen."

Gabriel nodded. "*Senhor* Ribeiro was very pleased with the arrangement."

"But what about—"

Micah stopped her. "There must always be a concession, Ms. Parvaneh. You've forged a powerful new alliance. Our employer will be very proud upon your return."

The driver's voice cut off Parvaneh's response.

"*Por favor*," he called, "you may load the vehicle now."

The bodyguard stepped aside as we entered. Micah took the passenger seat and I slid behind the driver again, completely unnoticed by Parvaneh. She seemed lost in thought, oblivious to Gabriel and me flanking her.

The Suburban pulled forward, and our driver addressed us as he ascended the ramp spiraling upward to ground level. "We will arrive at Le Chateaux Mer within twenty minutes. A second vehicle will deliver your possessions once we arrive. I am sorry for the inconvenience, but this is how our employer prefers to receive his visitors."

"We understand," Parvaneh said, "and trust in the protection of your organization's security plan."

We reached the street level and pulled into a gap in traffic, cruising easily with the row of cars between stoplights. The streets looked different now, storefront lights coming on as windows glowed against the waning sun. People circulated freely among the sidewalks, carrying shopping bags as bicyclists zipped between them.

We reentered the same tunnel, though rather than returning to the ocean road we turned southwest. Eventually I caught sight of the enormous lake I'd circumvented with Reilly that morning—we were passing back into Ipanema, with Leblon and our hotel now minutes away. Turning to the south, we crossed back into the upscale shopping district.

Suddenly the twirling reflection of red lights blazed across the store windows.

A rush of flight instinct hit me, forged over the course

of a hundred illegal BASE jumps that remained fixed in my system no matter the setting.

Micah asked, "Is this a problem?"

"Routine," our driver replied. "We have an arrangement, as you must imagine."

I looked between them at two police vehicles parked on the curb three cars in front of us. A single officer stood in the street, checking the identification of a driver before waving him forward.

Micah slowly unfastened his seatbelt and pulled it off his lap, and I followed his lead as the car in front of us was checked. After the officer waved us forward, our driver rolled his window down. The thick plate of ballistic glass descended eight inches before it stopped in place.

The officer seemed annoyed at this irregularity. "*Identificação, por favor.*"

The driver seemed to be no stranger to random police checkpoints. One hand remained on the steering wheel in a nonaggressive posture while his other had opened a billfold by the time he was asked for identification.

"*Boa noite, oficial,*" he replied, holding his identification still. "*Missão diplomatica. Por ordem do governador.*"

The police officer peered in through the partially open window, glancing over the identification before his eyes settled on Parvaneh in the center back seat.

Instead of waving us forward, he called, "*Saia do carro.*"

Gabriel murmured quietly, "He says to get out of the car."

Our driver held his billfold back up. "*Não há problema. Chame o escritório do governador.*"

"Call the governor's office," Gabriel continued.

The officer drew his pistol and shouted, "*Largue a arma!*"

"Drop the gun—"

The first shot hit the driver in the head.

For a split second I was back in the car with Karma as we were ambushed. I grabbed the back of her head and threw her face down between her knees, covering her body with mine as the cop angled sideways to acquire her in his sights.

But Micah was already out of his seat, straddling the center console, his head low against the exposed ballistic glass, punching the accelerator with his left foot.

The next seconds were a pummeling gauntlet—our truck glanced off a vehicle to the left, and then smashed off another to the right, as the snare drum impact of bullets popped into the glass and pinged off the armored surfaces. We swung left a final time before the Suburban's right side hit something with a screeching bang of crushed metal that brought us to a halt in a grinding, low-speed collision.

I leaned up, and Parvaneh flung me off her. Micah's shoulders moved slowly. He was dazed but not shot, slumped over the dash with his left foot mashed on the accelerator, our tires spinning in place.

I grabbed his arm and shook him hard. "Can you drive?"

He let up on the gas as his head rose slowly from the dash. He mumbled, "Yeah...I..."

We'd smashed into a parked car, our Suburban frozen at a 45-degree angle at a T-intersection. With him straddling the console and the dead man in the driver's seat, I couldn't climb into the front without exiting the armored confines of our truck.

"Open your door," I yelled to Micah, stumbling out of

the vehicle and slamming my door shut to shield Parvaneh.

The streets were pandemonium. While the shot that killed the driver could have been mistaken for a car back-firing, those that followed it as our armored Suburban blindly careened through a stoplight had incited a wave of panic. Oncoming cars blocked by our Suburban were abandoned as terrified men and women darted to build-ings, screaming amid the whizzing hisses and pops of incoming bullets from multiple shooters behind us.

I heaved open the driver's door as Micah struggled to recover his bearings. The dead chauffeur was behind him, staring at me, his face marred by a single red dot on the bridge of his nose like a third eye. Bullets were hitting our truck, barking off the metal armor and popping into the ballistic glass. I grabbed the dead man's shoulders to pull him out, yanking at him twice before I registered that his seatbelt was still on. Micah was still clumsily trying to right himself, oblivious to my dilemma as I shoved him away and unfastened the driver's seatbelt by feel.

There were at least five shooters now, the closest gunfire drawing dangerously near—we'd only driven a few meters out of the kill zone. Our attackers were maneu-vering to overrun us, unopposed by a stunned and defenseless quarry.

Even amid my panicked surge of adrenaline, I strug-gled to wrench 230 pounds of deadweight out of the driver's seat as Micah pulled himself into the gap.

The driver's body tilted sideways before gravity took over and he fell facedown onto the pavement, his billfold tumbling beside him. On the back of his head was a bloody, cratered exit wound the size of my fist.

I instinctively pocketed the billfold, my peripheral

vision registering the spark of a round ricocheting off the pavement three feet to my left. Rolling the driver onto his back in a desperate search for the pistol Micah and I had spotted, I ripped open his suit jacket.

Beneath his left armpit, a brown leather shoulder holster pinned a Beretta 92 to his side.

I thumbed the retention snap and drew the pistol out, flicking the decocker off as I whirled toward the sound of gunfire. A human form rounded the Suburban's rear bumper and I began squeezing the trigger as fast as I possibly could, the first assessment of my target occurring after it dropped from my sights after six rounds.

A dying cop sprawled out on the ground a few meters away, writhing in his final moments, hands clutched to a throat expelling blood like a fire hydrant.

"*GET IN!*" Micah yelled.

The back door was open beside me, held in place by Parvaneh's outstretched arm.

I dove into the seat beside her as Micah reversed in a wide, curving arc. Grabbing the door handle with both hands, I hauled it shut as our Suburban came broadside to the kill zone and received a final flurry of bullet impacts.

Micah threw the transmission into drive and punched the accelerator, the engine roaring with effort as the heavy vehicle gained momentum away from the ambush. He closed the ballistic glass of the driver's window to seal the unprotected gap in our armor, quieting the whistle of wind.

"We won't get away," Gabriel blurted. "David's a cop killer."

Micah's voice was steel. "We stop, we die. Did you get a phone off the driver?"

"Just his wallet," I said.

"Well we can't use that to call the fucking helicopter, now can we?"

Gabriel's panicked voice again. "We need to turn ourselves in and let the Handler's lawyers deal with it. Otherwise we'll be killed."

Parvaneh spoke for the first time since the driver got shot.

"If you discuss surrender again, I'll save them the trouble of killing you. Give Micah directions back to the hotel. We're getting back to our people and calling the Outfit helicopter."

Gabriel looked terrified, but his words came quickly.

"Two blocks ahead. Take a left."

Micah swerved the Suburban into a parking lot to pass a row of traffic, and then crossed two lanes to cut through the intersection amidst the squealing of brakes and angry objections of car horns.

Gabriel said, "Left here."

Micah complied and then aborted the maneuver mid-turn, speeding forward through the crosswalk instead. I looked left to see a roadblock of two stationary cop cars blocking the way in the distance.

I slid the Beretta into my waistband. "They've already blocked off the hotel. Go the opposite way."

Gabriel turned to me, alarmed. "North? Why?"

"All we need is enough distance to make a phone call."

Micah said, "He's right—take us to the emergency landing zone at Jockey Club. We'll dismount and find a phone there."

"Take the next right."

The following turn revealed sparse traffic. Micah swung the car perpendicular to our lane to cut off a car behind us, a near-crash into the adjacent building avoided as he reversed the wheel at the last second and repeated the process on the opposite side. He repeated another sharp S-turn, creating further gaps in traffic as progressively alarmed drivers braked and allowed us to gain distance.

"Five blocks to a right turn on Route Black—Jockey Club is just on the other side."

Flashing red lights appeared in front of us as a police car braked to a halt at an intersection ahead, blocking our lane. Another joined it a moment later, parking end-to-end as the officers scrambled out and took cover behind their vehicles.

There was nowhere for us to turn.

"Seatbelts on," Micah said evenly, buckling his as I did the same. He sped down a turn lane to cut around a trio of cars, flinging us back into our original lane as bullets began pocking the windshield. Micah slowed just before impact, and then held a steady speed as the officers dove toward the sidewalk. Our Suburban's bumper impacted the rear quarter panel of a cop car, pivoting the vehicle around its engine block and out of our way. Micah accelerated our truck forward and out of the police perimeter.

Gabriel said, "Four more blocks till Route Black."

We plunged forward, racing down the length of street temporarily empty from the cops' blockage of outbound traffic. Every momentarily empty surface became an extension of Micah's racetrack: turn lanes, sidewalks, and the opposite side of the road. He began blasting the horn as a stoplight approached, speeding through it on a green light.

"Three blocks to go."

He used the bumper to burrow our way between two

vehicles, thumping them aside before racing through a yellow light. A convertible making a turn ahead stopped suddenly, the sharp screech of his brakes halting his car inches from impact.

"Two more blocks."

We were screaming along now, Micah blasting the horn as he plowed through cars with fleeting scrapes on both sides. He threw us onto the curb to pass a car, then accelerated past a red light.

"One block. Micah MICAH—"

A white car made a last-ditch attempt to speed through the intersection ahead of us, and the Suburban's front end plummeted as Micah stomped the brakes. I threw an arm across Parvaneh's chest, my last memory before impact a snapshot view of our Suburban reflected back at us from the sedan's side windows.

The crash jarred me forward against the seatbelt, my head narrowly missing the seat in front of me as our rear wheels left the ground. Our back end spun left and then slammed down unevenly as we plunged into a light pole.

A sudden jolt brought us to a complete stop, scrambling my thoughts like a kick to the skull. For seconds my brain ceased to function, the first coherent thought post-crash being the repugnant chemical smell. My mind was swimming. A light pole almost touched the windshield, our truck's hood crushed around it. Billowing white airbags deflated in the front seats. Parvaneh was beside me, tears sliding down her face, about to be run down by our pursuers and killed like Karma.

I unbuckled my seatbelt in what felt like slow motion, fumbling my hand across the door until I found the latch. Falling to the side, I slumped my shoulders across the door until my weight pushed it open.

I tumbled out of the vehicle and collapsed onto the pavement. Using the open door to pull myself up until I was shakily standing, I took in my surroundings.

Stationary headlights sliced through one another at awkward angles in the waning light as shadowy figures began to descend on the Suburban from vehicles abandoned in disarray.

The nearest man approached from his stopped Mercedes with hands extended, an apparent effort to calm me until the ambulance arrived. All sound was lost against an earsplitting ringing, my reaction occurring with the groggy detachment of seeing it through someone else's eyes.

The Beretta was suddenly in my hand, cracking itself savagely across the man's face before waving in a sideways arc that repelled the figures around me. The man I'd struck recoiled from the head impact, turning to retreat as I grabbed the back of his shirt and pressed my barrel into the base of his neck.

I threw him onto the hood of his car, holding him there until the rumble assured me the vehicle was still running.

"Phone," I yelled at him. "*Teléfono.*"

He pulled out a flip phone, a precious lifeline to the Outfit helicopter that I shoved in my pocket with my free hand. Then I tossed him to the side, carving a wide semicircle around me with the Beretta to defend my prize, a dying scavenger desperate to claim a chance scrap.

I dropped the barrel as it crossed Parvaneh.

Her head was low, body crouched at the waist as Micah raced her toward me and into the backseat of the Mercedes. I scrambled around the hood and into the passenger seat as Micah slid behind the wheel, putting the car in drive. Forgotten in the melee, Gabriel scuttled into the backseat a second before Micah sped our new vehicle out of the chaos of the intersection.

I regained my senses and braced for another impact.

We raced down a sidewalk past the standstill traffic surrounding the crash, rumbling into the opposing lane and accelerating to a speed that seemed suicidal in an urban sprawl. Just as the lit windows and streetlights couldn't have whizzed by any faster out my window, Micah swerved back toward the sidewalk, applied a screeching surge of brakes, and very nearly missed clipping the corner curb to complete a right turn onto a six-lane divided road.

He slammed the brakes behind a car as other vehicles closed in around us, and within seconds we had melted into the traffic crawling forward.

No cops in sight.

Retrieving the phone in my pocket, I thrust it back toward Gabriel. "Call the helicopter."

He snatched the phone. "Take the next left off this road. Jockey Club is a few blocks away." A pause. "David, this phone is passcode-protected."

"Start guessing," Micah snapped. Then, more calmly, "Parvaneh, are you hurt?"

I looked back at her, half expecting to see Karma in her final moment.

But Parvaneh's face was tilted down, tendrils of hair hanging over eyes that stared forward, glinting with the rippling passage of streetlights. Unmistakable rage. She spoke three words.

"Was it Ribeiro?"

Her voice was dark, gritty, brimming with a visceral hatred that, even under our current circumstances, and even to me, seemed dangerous. No matter how polished and courteous she seemed in the light of day, she held a high position within a criminal organization whose magnitude and proportions I was just beginning to grasp.

Micah said, "All that matters right now is getting you back to Langley."

I looked to him, then Parvaneh—no response, both expressionless. Apart from being a four-hour drive from my Virginia hometown, Langley was ubiquitously used as a reference to the CIA. My thoughts darted to the American flag suspended from the framework of the Complex hangar.

Who were these people?

The flickering red hue of police light bars appeared on the road in front of us, and the traffic came to a complete halt. A second later I saw police officers advancing between cars toward us, guns raised, peering inside the windows of stopped cars.

"Fuck," Micah whispered.

I buckled my seatbelt as he spun the wheel left, mounting the median curb and cutting between two trees as traffic in the opposite lanes braked to avoid him. Our car thumped back down onto the far side of the road as Micah completed his U-turn, accelerating westbound away from the roadblock.

I turned to see the cops through the rear windshield, their figures glowing in the headlights of idling traffic. They weren't shooting at us, though their reaction was something infinitely more dangerous—they were speaking into their radios.

Micah's focus was consumed by driving, and I stepped in to fill the strategic gap.

"We can't outrun police radios. Or spike strips. We've got to find a place where the cops won't follow."

Gabriel replied, "There's nowhere they won't follow us."

"What about a favela?" I asked.

He fell silent, and Micah latched onto this uncertainty like a pit bull. "Goddammit, Gabriel, what about a favela?"

Turning to look at Gabriel's stunned face, I caught sight of more police lights approaching from behind.

I said, "Gabriel, you're going to give Micah directions to a place where the cops won't follow us."

"I don't take orders from you."

"You do now. I've got nine bullets left. If we get stopped, the first is yours."

"Closest favela is Rocinha. Gangs there are worse than cops."

I made eye contact with Parvaneh. "All we need is a phone. We can survive anywhere but here for ten minutes until the chopper arrives."

"He's right," Micah said.

The next voice was hers. "Gabriel, take us there."

"Fine. Take the next right."

We turned onto a narrow one-way street lined with parked cars. This couldn't be the correct road—the sidewalks were planted with ferns and trees that blocked my view of tall buildings rising into the night. Not the slightest hint of poverty to be seen.

I checked my side view mirror and saw a single cop car make the turn to follow us, joined a moment later by a second.

"Two cops in pursuit," I said.

Gabriel shouted, "Left at the intersection."

Micah proceeded without slowing in the least, waiting

until the four-way was imminent before cutting into the far-right lane and standing up on the brakes. He ripped the wheel left, yanking the handbrake as our back end swung right. Our sideways drift brought us broadside within inches of a pickup before Micah dropped the handbrake, punching the gas to shoot forward again.

We sped down a four-lane hardball, still being pursued by the two police vehicles. The road merged into two lanes, and then a single one-way channel so tight that I thought my side view mirror would clip a row of parked cars as Micah followed Gabriel's directions.

Soon there was no longer any traffic moving forward, and I spun to gain an unobstructed view of the two cop cars keeping pace with us. Untamed vegetation closed in on us as we wound uphill.

When we crossed into the favela, I knew it at once.

The boundary between the city and the favela was more defined than any international border in the world —paved streets and lit storefronts relinquished their hold to a narrow dirt road threading into a ghostly kingdom of shanties.

Our headlights fell on graffiti-sprayed walls extending upward to multi-tiered balconies until a tangled spider web of wires suspended over the narrow street obscured the view.

The police response told me everything I needed to know about where we were entering—their collective flashing lights stopped at the threshold and then disappeared altogether as Micah threaded our car forward into the darkness.

ESCAPE

Omnia mors aequat

-Death makes all things equal

4

Micah continued piloting the Mercedes up a steep incline, the narrow road threading past more dilapidated structures. Our headlights illuminated a jumbled mess of mildew-stained concrete, sheet metal, and steel drums. Giant canvas sacks and piles of dirt leaned against walls, decrepit cars fell into decay atop streets and sidewalks, but the entire uninhabitable portrait of abject poverty was nonetheless brimming with masses of people packed into every space.

"Park as soon as you can," Gabriel said. "Territory will become more contested between gangs the further we go."

I asked, "You sure these people have phones?"

"Internet too. Everything is illegally siphoned from Rio. Electricity, water, everything. Look up."

He nodded toward the tangles of black wire stretched between the second stories of the favela. Our view suddenly became blocked by a mass of people rushing uphill, flowing past us like a school of fish that quickly slowed our progress to a crawl.

Parvaneh asked, "What's going on out there?"

"I have no clue," Gabriel said, "but we're better off in the crowd than outside it. We need to get away from this car."

Micah looked over at me from the driver's seat. "Give me the gun."

"I can shoot as well as you."

We pulled into an open section of road, edging in as much as the tight dirt path allowed. He killed the engine and turned to face me.

"Maybe you can, maybe you can't. But we're not betting her life on it."

I handed him the Beretta.

He snatched it from my hand, checking the chamber and magazine before sliding it into his belt. Pulling his suit jacket over it, he said, "Everyone stick with Gabriel. Let him do the talking. Let's move."

We exited the vehicle to a symphony of noise: thumping samba bass notes, barking dogs, babies crying in every direction at once. I scanned for threats—everywhere I looked were thin metal doors, chain link, chicken wire, and dim lights casting a murky glow into the maze we'd just entered. Urine, rotting garbage, and fried food melded into a choking stench as the vast crowd of people rushed up the street, oblivious to Gabriel calling out for help.

Finally, a man in his twenties stopped. The subsequent flurry of shared Portuguese was punctuated by Gabriel trading cash for a cell phone, the two of them glancing at the screen in confusion before the man shrugged and took his phone back, keeping the money and walking uphill.

Gabriel turned to us. "He said police are blocking the streets and checking everyone going in or out. And there's no phone reception—someone has already shut down the cell towers."

Micah glowered at him. "Find a landline. Now."

Gabriel turned in a circle, examining our surroundings before shoving through the crowd toward a storefront.

A tall man with a pencil moustache who was smoking a cigarette with aplomb stood by the entryway.

"*Linha fixa*?" Gabriel asked him.

The vendor waved his cigarette inside as if he'd been expecting us. "*Claro, claro, pode entrar.*"

We stepped into the shop. The interior reminded me of being in Afghanistan more than anything I'd yet seen in South America: three claustrophobically tight walls covered floor-to-ceiling in wares ranging from clothes to junk food, cigarettes to shoes. Like a fern growing among rocks, the entrepreneurial spirit resulted in retail stores stocking, selling, and trading anything and everything the most poverty-stricken environment had to offer.

Gabriel took the cordless phone being offered by the vendor, then pressed a button and held it to his ear.

He shook his head at Micah.

The vendor took the phone from him and pressed the power button, listening to the receiver before speaking apologetically in Portuguese.

Gabriel spoke quietly. "Landline and cell reception have been cut. We're fucked, Micah."

"Shut up. Ask him where we can find a radio. CB, ham radio, whatever's around."

The man shook his head in response to Gabriel's inquiry.

Micah asked Gabriel, "Can we leave the favela on foot?"

"Cops are blocking roads to the east, and we'll never make it to the west side of Rocinha alive. The north and south are blocked by mountains too steep to climb."

Undeterred, Micah gestured to the metal roll-down door above us. "Close. Close up."

The shopkeeper gave Micah an eyebrow-raised glance as if reproaching a schoolboy for talking back and then rubbed the fingertips of one hand together. "*Dinheiro.*"

Gabriel sighed. "You need me to translate that?"

"We'll pay. And tell him we're buying clothes, jackets, and shoes for all of us." As Gabriel began to translate, Micah added, "Food, bottled water. And newspapers."

Gabriel began thumbing through a wad of bills. The vendor's eyes dipped to the cash and he nonchalantly closed the roll-down door to ensconce us beneath two bare light bulbs.

Micah addressed all of us. "Lose the suits. Put on whatever fits."

I grabbed a windbreaker off a hanger beside me, and then noticed that Parvaneh was standing a few feet away with her feet shoulder-width apart, unbuttoning her blouse to expose a white bra and a long, lean abdomen the same olive shade as her face. Her physique was toned, athletic, the subtle definition of her abdominals visible even in the store's poor lighting.

"David," Micah said through gritted teeth.

He and Gabriel had already turned away. Even the vendor had reluctantly faced the wall.

I gave a repentant shrug and turned away from Parvaneh. "I've already saved her ass by getting us a gun and a car. At least one of us is keeping an eye on the primary."

Micah's face visibly reddened. He slapped Gabriel on the arm and pointed to the vendor.

"And tell him I need to buy his lighter."

* * *

Micah finished lighting the last of three fires to complete a triangle of burning newspaper and trash on a flat roof less than twenty meters from the rooftop shed where Parvaneh and Gabriel were safely tucked away. The sun had set in the hours since our race from the police, the air now tinged with a cool, comfortable dampness.

I knelt beside him in the darkness. "Rio's a big city, Micah."

"This favela is a much smaller piece."

"If your people figure out we're here."

"They already know that much from the intel network, not to mention monitoring the police scanners. They're looking for us right now. The surveillance plane will find our signal fires within the hour if we're lucky. At worst, three to four hours until they spot us."

We'd successfully donned a haphazard array of street clothes. They fit into our surroundings only slightly better than the business attire Micah had added to the flames, fearful that the vendor would try to sell it and betray our passage. Upon exiting the shop, we quickly found that the only way to escape the sweltering masses of people in the favela was to travel as far upward as we could go.

Even then, the small, empty patch of corrugated iron roof that we now occupied had taken thirty minutes of negotiating noisy balconies and rooftop water tanks to find.

I asked, "So what happens when the plane finds our

signal fires? The Outfit helicopter breaks every speed record in the book to get here?"

His chin bobbed in the firelight. "Count on it."

"Just blazing in, shooting anyone around us?"

Micah spoke slowly, quietly. "That's the lowest-profile ending we'll see."

"What's the highest-profile ending?"

"You know by now what he's capable of. What do you think he's going to do, David?"

I studied Micah's face, his features lit by the orange glow that sharpened the lines and made him look much older than he had in the light of day. I responded, "If he were going to invade the favela, he'd be doing it right now."

"He doesn't have enough men here for a raid. But you can bet the entire Outfit is on their way to Rio as we speak. Given the time it'll take to mobilize them, and the flight from the Complex to Brazil, that would put their invasion at nightfall tomorrow."

"He cares that much about his ambassador?"

"He and I have that much in common." He looked at me quickly, adding, "What's your excuse?"

I felt my anger rising. After my vision of Karma and then seeing Parvaneh very nearly meet the same fate, I was nearly quaking with rage.

"Hey, genius, I'm not the one who let her waltz into that truck. You couldn't see that death trap from a mile away?"

"Her judgment isn't mine to control. But her survival is."

"You think I don't care about that too?"

"That's not the same as keeping her from getting hurt."

I planted a fist against the gritty iron surface below

me, taking a breath to calm myself. "I don't understand what you mean."

"That much is clear."

"If you expect me to be better informed, you could start by explaining why I was sent here in the first place."

"If I had the authority to disclose that, you'd listen to me a lot better than you are now."

"Do you have the authority to tell me about Langley?"

His expression solidified into resolute silence.

"Yeah, I didn't forget about that little CIA reference you made back in the car. Is Parvaneh an Agency asset, or is the whole organization a front for Langley?"

My words caused a seismic shift in his demeanor. His eyes turned black in the firelight, his mouth parting to breathe as his voice lowered. "If I hear that word begin to leave your lips one more time, I'm going to break your jaw before you finish it."

I shook my head in disgust. "Everyone's been eager to threaten me. I'm curious why no one has just blown my head off by now."

He stood and brushed the ashes from his thighs.

"Make sure the fires stay lit. I'll check on you in an hour."

He stalked away, moving quietly to the rooftop shed where Parvaneh and Gabriel waited.

I watched him leave, trying to make sense of the interaction. The mention of Langley had struck a nerve that I wanted to understand, but it didn't matter much to my present situation—the Handler was waiting to kill me upon my return, and whether he was sponsored by the US Government didn't change the fact that I needed to assassinate him. The Indian's life had already been lost in this game, and mine was going to follow in short order. But Ian's hadn't, at least not yet.

I moved to a rickety overhang of sheet metal, looking back to ensure it would allow me to observe the fires while remaining hidden in shadow. The delta of flame burned crisply, though I questioned the effectiveness of our fires despite Micah's confidence that the aircraft could spot them. My nighttime view from the roof revealed a dense expanse of favela that glittered with outdoor cooking flames, poorly lit balconies, and steel drums containing the blaze of fire.

On a quiet night I may have been able to hear the surveillance plane circling in the black sky overhead. As it was, the constant ringing in my ears took a distant second to rhythmic bass notes and periodic laughter within the brick walls all around me, and honking motorcycles in the tight streets below, the collective throb of tightly-packed civilization punctuated by barking dogs. I gathered my knees between my elbows, my back beginning to ache dully, its first objection to the Suburban crash.

The lights of a distant balcony were extinguished as my thoughts shifted to the identity of our aggressors, whether cop or otherwise, though that might not matter a terrible amount to me at present. As I kept the signal fires in my periphery to retain what night vision I could, I thought about the greater issue looming in the midnight of my future—my fate upon returning from Brazil.

The helicopter was a few hours out at most. I'd be executed at my next meeting with the Handler, and if I didn't find a way to kill him first, Ian would recklessly continue his assassination schemes until he got slain in the process. Our team and Karma would be unavenged, and the course of events from my exile, to Africa, to South

America and back would represent little more than an elaborate exercise in futility.

Another balcony went dark, followed by the abrupt cessation of a stereo blasting samba music. I rose to a crouch beneath the sheet metal over my head, a great tingling ripple of goose bumps spreading across my neck.

The rapid-fire barking of dogs erupted a few blocks away and then went silent.

I burst out of my hidden alcove and raced toward the rooftop shed, stumbling over a pile of scrap wood and recovering my bearings as I plunged through the darkness. The shed was ten feet distant when a black shape appeared to my left and arrested all forward momentum with a sudden blow across my chest.

My body spun in a controlled descent, and as I slammed to the ground Micah's face appeared over mine.

"What are you doing?" he whispered.

"We've got to move her. Now. Something's coming for us from the east."

His hesitation only lasted half a breath before he was gone, his face replaced by an empty black sky.

I rolled over and scrambled to my feet, seeing that Micah was already pulling Parvaneh from the shed. Joined by his hand on her wrist, they broke into a run toward an edge of the roof that Micah must have plotted as his primary escape route. Gabriel stumbled out of the shed and followed them, and I had almost caught up to the trio when they disappeared off the edge of the roof.

I jumped off without looking, my stomach leaping to my throat amid the knowledge that to lose sight of them was a death sentence that wouldn't particularly trouble any of them.

The fall was short, ending in a lower balcony that I

landed on just in time to see Micah kicking open a flimsy door, gun drawn as he pulled Parvaneh into the harsh fluorescent light of a home scarcely bigger than the average American living room.

We raced through a tiny dwelling where a family dined on the single couch, the teenage father leaping up and shielding an even younger woman with two toddlers.

"*Desculpa, desculpa*," Gabriel yelled, a single yellow bill of currency fluttering in his wake.

We were gone as quickly as we had arrived, Micah flinging open the far door and disappearing down a shoddy staircase. I leapt down the stairs after them until we arrived at ground level, where Micah led us past a row of erratically parked cars along the narrow, crumbling street. After clambering over a pile of loose brick, we slipped between unfinished concrete surfaces and followed a tight footpath to a short wall.

Micah climbed over first, assisting Parvaneh as I trailed behind them. From there we took a wild route through alleys and switchbacks threading deeper into the maze, sporadic groups of people smoking and drinking and dancing to stereos, trash packed into the crevices lining the space between buildings.

Micah found an outdoor staircase leading up, and we climbed past landing after landing until it would rise no higher. We stepped onto a covered balcony wrapping past lit windows and hurried toward a rickety ladder leaned against a wall. Clambering up its quaking height, we arrived at a rooftop and slipped under an awning of bed sheets strung above us.

Kneeling in the shadows, I saw Micah scanning across the other rooftops until he found our signal. No one spoke for a few minutes of panting breath as our pulses returned to normal. The three fires continued to burn amid the irregular lighting pooled in the fissures of the labyrinth.

Finally, Micah whispered, "If that helicopter lands at the signal while we're sitting here because you got spooked for no reason, I'm going to kill you."

I shook my head. "Something was coming for us."

"How do you know?"

"I just knew. Lights started going out. Music stopped."

"It's getting late. Of course people shut off their lights. Gabriel?"

Gabriel sighed. "The favelas are no different than any other city. This is all... normal, Micah. I don't know what else to tell you."

"So we exposed ourselves and fled from our signal for nothing."

Parvaneh touched Micah's arm. "What do we do now?"

"We make our way back and hope the helicopter doesn't come before we get there."

"Micah," I said as firmly as I could without raising my voice, "I've been to war in three countries now. Brazil will make four. And I'm telling you, something was coming for us."

He drew closer to me, his face a black shadow.

"I don't care if you think you're a war hero."

"I never said—"

"You have zero credibility here. This isn't the military, no matter how much you want it to be."

Parvaneh spoke to me. "If Micah says we go back, we go back. His experience means more than your instinct, David."

"My instinct told you not to get in that car. How many

times do I have to save you before you get over my shitty haircut?"

"Micah's experience got us out with our lives."

Micah grabbed my arm. "You're not making the decisions here. We go back and—"

Parvaneh gasped. "Look!"

Following her eyes toward the signal, I saw the fires glowing just as before, their collective light dimming as the piles of wood, trash, and clothes slowly burned out.

"What?" Micah asked.

She replied, "Can't you see?"

I stared at the signal, unable to discern what she was talking about.

Then I saw the man.

At first he was just a shadow, but gradually the signal fires silhouetted his figure. He was moving precisely, tactically, his steps preceded by the suppressor of a rifle as a second man appeared behind him.

Gabriel asked, "Are they from the Outfit?"

"Not a chance," Micah responded. "The Outfit would have come by helicopter."

The second man's head turned to reveal the insect-like profile of a night vision device suspended over his eyes, and then he continued moving until a third man passed into the light.

Parvaneh asked, "What if they had to insert by ground, Micah?"

"Outfit shooters would be treating it like a hostage rescue. They'd be white-lighting the rooftop and calling for us, knowing the helicopter was a few minutes away."

Gabriel offered, "Maybe the ambush wasn't Ribeiro. Maybe his people are trying to help us."

"Ribeiro's people wouldn't know our recovery signal."

Gabriel replied, "Unless they were working with the Handler to find us."

"The Handler wouldn't trust anyone else to recover a delegation. He'd send the Outfit."

Almost in unison, the three men kicked the burning piles apart, stomping the flame before vanishing into the darkness as quickly as they had appeared.

I asked, "Think the store owner ratted us out?"

"We didn't set up the signal anywhere near his shop."

"What about a tracking device?" I offered. "We took the driver's gun."

"If there was a tracking device, they would have followed us here, not to the other roof."

Gabriel sounded fearful. "Maybe they got lucky."

"There's no way they found that rooftop that quickly by accident. We've only been in the favela for a few hours."

I looked up. "I know how they found us."

"How?" Parvaneh asked.

"They've got an aircraft searching for our signal just like our guys have been. Whoever's trying to kill us just found it sooner. Come on, Micah, I thought you were the bodyguard here. Why do I have to think all this shit up?"

"There's no way," Parvaneh objected. "That's too—"

I cut her off. "Think about it. First, we drove into a police ambush, and then the landlines and cell towers get knocked out. Now the cops have barricaded us in the favela, and a kill team arrives at our beacon almost as soon as we get it lit. Someone besides the Handler has a surveillance plane overhead looking for us."

"Could they know what our signal was?" she asked Micah.

He frowned. "Not unless they had an inside man, and

even then, very few people know what the recovery signal would be for any given mission."

"That's beside the point," I said. "We can't leave the favela, we can't signal our plane, and three men are hunting us with automatic weapons, and that's before we take the local criminals into account. We're going to need more than one pistol to defend ourselves—we need better guns."

"What we need is a radio," Micah said. "If we can get our hands on an advanced civilian or military-grade radio, I can raise the Complex shooters on the emergency frequency. We've got plenty of cash. Where can we get both, Gabriel?"

He shook his head mournfully. "Drug traffickers. High-level guys will definitely have guns, maybe radios."

"How do we find them?"

"The lieutenants are living as extravagantly as they can. Finding them won't be the hard part."

"What will?"

Gabriel helplessly shrugged. "Being able to state our request before they kill us."

I pounded three times on the metal door, the noise reverberating until it echoed to silence.

After a few seconds without response, I pounded on the door again.

"Patience," Gabriel scolded. "These are serious people."

I took a long breath, the rising sun's first rays providing a circadian reprieve from the exhaustion of a mostly sleepless night. Turning to look at Gabriel, I observed the downside of sunrise: it exposed how ridiculous he looked. He wore a mishmash of hastily purchased clothes: ill-fitting tennis shoes, shorts, and a sleeveless athletic shirt that revealed arms that hadn't seen the inside of a gym since his last day of high school tennis.

My appearance wasn't much better, I supposed, between my shaved head and the pièce de résistance of my favela wardrobe, a thin white windbreaker that I hoped could partially conceal newly acquired weapons. I'd have to talk my way through a black-market negotiation before being able to test the jacket's efficacy—we'd left our sole pistol with Micah and Parvaneh.

I pointed at the letters *ADA* spray-painted on the door. "What does that mean?"

"*Amigos dos Amigos*," he whispered. "Friends of Friends."

"Not very sinister. What are you so worked up about?"

"They will kill for nothing. Their justice is lead, David. Or worse, the *microondas*."

"*Microondas*, eh? Sounds innocent enough."

"This means 'microwave.' They place men within a stack of tires, soak them in gasoline, and then set them on—"

A crudely welded slot in the door slid open, and beyond it a pair of dark eyes watched us.

"Fire?" I guessed.

Gabriel smiled at the slot, and then said quickly, "*Bom dia, senhor—*"

"*O que que tu quer*," a voice responded in a thick Brazilian accent.

They launched into a back-and-forth exchange in Portuguese, and I didn't need a native fluency to tell that Gabriel was losing.

"Enough," I said. "What's he saying?"

"He says we can get guns anywhere. He wants to know why we came here."

"We're looking for real hardware. Submachine guns, something we can conceal under a jacket. And radios. We've got enough cash to make it worth his boss's while, and he can tell by my skin and accent that I'm not a fucking cop. Tell him."

Another exchange in Portuguese. The sun was rising and the streets grew more crowded by the second, but the door remained closed as they continued to talk.

I interrupted, "Tell him we walk in five seconds. He can have our money, or his competitors can."

Gabriel spoke quickly. The set of eyes behind the door shifted from Gabriel to me, then back again, before the slot closed. The rusty shriek of metal on metal sounded from within before the door swung open on creaking hinges.

In the short distance between the door and an inner building encapsulated by the perimeter wall stood four skinny, shirtless teenage boys with red handkerchiefs tied below their eyes. I looked from weapon to weapon in their hands—two AK-47 assault rifles, an MP-5 submachine gun, and a pump-action shotgun.

"Good," I concluded. "Looks like we came to the right place."

Small hands frisked us with a thoroughness that surprised me before the child sentries closed the gate and led us through an open doorway.

The building's interior was a bizarrely clean and modern space, the destitution of the slum suspended amid a micro-universe of ersatz wealth. Clean white walls surrounded us as we walked atop gleaming floor tiles, passing between glass coffee tables and ample furniture overlooking giant flat-screen televisions with speakers wired in every direction. The wall beside us held a mural-sized painting of a woman I presumed to be a Brazilian pop star, her crudely painted face marred by a bullet hole in the cheek.

We passed into an open courtyard to the sound of a woman shrieking.

I looked over in alarm only to see one bikini-clad teenage girl violently shoving another in the early morning light. The victim fell backward, splashing into the waist-deep water of a swimming pool. Her impact disturbed a flotilla of empty liquor bottles that clanked against the plastic boundaries of a pool that would have been comically small in any other setting, but at present seemed an ostentatious display of incalculable wealth.

Over the roof at the edge of the courtyard, I caught my first close-up, daylight view of a hilltop steeped with shanties. Their dilapidated surfaces were layered with an ingenuity that was almost hard to perceive with the untrained eye. What appeared at first to be total chaos was, in the next second, ordered into an imaginative array of vertical expansion, the collective mass clinging to hills that most occupants of the civilized world would consider too steep to walk.

Before I could consider this further, the prod of a barrel in my spine pushed me forward into an open room bordering the courtyard. As we entered, three boys who had been lounging on sofas leapt to their feet and snatched rifles from the seat beside them. Across a coffee table, in a recliner from which he didn't stand, was a black man of twenty years at best, no shirt and not an ounce of fat on his body, with a Glock stuffed in the waistband of his shorts and a walkie-talkie on the table to his front. His feet bore brand-new red sneakers, one of which was propped up against the edge of the table as he watched us, unimpressed.

"*Senta*," one of the armed boys said, shoving Gabriel and me onto a sofa whose fabric surfaces smelled like they'd been marinated in pot. The ringleader's eyes looked on edge, and the others took their cue from him, mirroring a vague anxiety that seemed unrelated to our arrival.

The ringleader began speaking in rapid-fire Portuguese, his words translated in a low murmur by Gabriel. "I am Enzo, and I have authority for this district straight from the *Mestre*—this means Master, the ADA drug lord that controls most of Rocinha—and I don't need permission to kill you for coming here. Do we have an understanding?"

I nodded.

Enzo leaned back in his chair and spoke as Gabriel continued translating, his eyes fixed on Enzo's mouth. "Last night we lost all phone service and an army of cops blocked off the entrances to my favela. I've got product I can't move, and I'm talking to my people on this piece of shit." Enzo picked up the walkie-talkie and flung it into my chest as I struggled to catch it. "This morning a gringo and a Brazilian pussy show up trying to buy guns. I do not believe in coincidence. I *do* believe that I have the source of all my problems sitting in front of me."

I held up the walkie-talkie and leaned forward. "Do you have bigger radios? Military, police-style."

Gabriel swung his pointed nose to me and translated Enzo's response. "If I had military radios I'd be using them. If there's a reason I should not kill you for coming here, it must be escaping my mind."

Another scream from a girl outside, followed by the splash of water and clanking of bottles as one of the boys snatched the walkie-talkie from me and returned it to the table. Enzo watched me intently.

I said, "We only want to buy a few guns and be on our way. We'll pay well."

"I take money anytime I want. I could make even more by slinging dust, until last night."

"We've got the keys to a Mercedes parked down the road."

"I can steal a Merc anytime I want."

I reached into my pocket, then froze as the guards in the room flinched to attention. Holding my free hand open, I slowly pulled out the driver's billfold, its surface crusted with his dried brown blood.

As the room collectively relaxed, I flipped it open to show the identification to Enzo. "Can you transport merchandise past police checkpoints with diplomatic immunity? Because this will allow you to do that."

One of the boys grabbed the billfold from me and handed it to Enzo, who examined the card with a poorly concealed expression of interest.

Then he tossed the billfold on the table, and Gabriel translated with an increasingly fearful voice, "I can kill you and take it, you get me? Know what? I'm going to do just that. Put these pussies in a microwave—"

Gabriel and I were jerked to our feet by the sentries around us. I threw a set of hands off me, and before the offending boy could raise his AK-47 I darted forward a step, and with lightning speed, slapped him hard across the face.

The boys grabbed me from behind as I yelled to Enzo, "You don't want to do that, *jefe*. Whatever happens to us happens to you."

He leapt to his feet and strode over to me, stopping a few feet away before barking a string of words.

Gabriel translated, "Too late to show your balls, gringo."

"You've got an American with diplomatic credentials. What do you think happens if I go missing?"

Enzo shook his head, and Gabriel translated, "Do not eat the meat where you earn your bread. This means that—"

"Don't shit where you eat," I cut Gabriel off. "What's his point?"

"We will not go missing. He can dump our bodies 'on the pavement' so we are found in the city."

I shook my head. "We didn't come here without insurance. We're desperate, not stupid. And our boss is neither."

Enzo's eyes were ablaze. "In this part of Rocinha, I *am* the boss."

I replied, "It's a wide world beyond the hills. That's the world that sent us, and that's where we'll return."

"You return nowhere unless I say you do. Who do you claim your boss to be?"

I thought of the Handler's golden eyes, his skewed nose hovering before me as I sat in the electric chair with water from the sponge dripping over my bare scalp and down my spine.

"If you don't know his name by now, I'd do my best to keep it that way. Now you'll get the money and the credentials whether you kill us or not. But a few guns that mean nothing to you will be the difference between whether you go to bed tonight as the ruler of your kingdom or whether you lie awake wondering if I was bluffing. And by the time you find out that I was not, it will be too late to save you. Or," I added, throwing my head toward the guards holding me from behind, "any of your people."

He fell under not just my stare, but also those of everyone around him, all looking to him to make sense of these events. The sum total of odd occurrences was too much for Enzo to ignore without some nagging suspicion that I wasn't completely lying. My sheer desperation in appearing in the first place indicated that there were unknown things beyond his realm that he shouldn't risk trifling with.

And in that moment of standoff, Gabriel displayed an untapped reserve of strength. His normally jumpy eyes were steady, the cartoonish features of his face frozen in solidarity with my effort to force Enzo's hand.

"Let me see the money," Enzo said at last.

His men released me, and I quickly handed over our prepared payment before Enzo could change his mind. The wad of bills represented the majority of our collective funds. Micah retained a small balance in the event we didn't return, along with our pistol, and I kept just enough stashed in my sock to procure food and water on our way back, should we live that long.

Enzo flipped through the equivalent of several thousand US dollars. His face indicated that he sensed something was amiss, though he remained uncertain whether to call my bluff. Either way, he wasn't going to lose face with his men by showing fear.

At last, he gave a nod at the amount of money we'd proffered, flicking his eyes toward a door in the corner.

Gabriel translated, "Let's go to the vault."

* * *

His stockpile was contained in a twenty-foot shipping container set against the back of the house, having been emplaced in the impossibly tight space by some marvel of third-world ingenuity that I didn't bother asking about. After removing a pair of locks and swinging the rusty doors open, his men aimed flashlights that cast indistinct shadows around the sweltering interior.

The back wall of the container was hidden behind a floor-to-ceiling mound of drugs packed into stuffed black trash bags and flat parcels wrapped with tape and cellophane of every color. Dozens of rifles and submachine guns leaned against the wall to my right, while a pile of pistols was heaped upon a small table.

My first glance revealed the vast majority of weapons to be useless to us. The variety of assault rifles had the range and accuracy suitable for ambushing a properly outfitted kill team, but I couldn't have every person on the stoop seeing a gringo running by with a full-size M-16 or AK-47. The need for balance of firepower and concealment narrowed my options considerably.

I saw a trio of MP5 submachine guns with retractable stocks and picked up one for inspection. Its heavy metal construction dated to the 1980s, free of the lightweight polymers, rail systems, lasers, and optics of modern military weapons. It fell into my hands easily: a cold, German, utilitarian weapon with simple iron sights, an 8.9-inch barrel, and the ability to reliably fire 9mm bullets from its stock thirty-round magazines as quickly as you could pull the trigger. With no range and no recoil, it would be useless at a distance but delightfully controllable inside a room.

I said, "For starters, I'll take all three of these."

Enzo shook his head, replying through Gabriel, "Those are hard to come by. You get two."

"The diplomatic identification alone is worth two. Together with the cash and the car, we should get all three MP5s and a fourth weapon. Plus some grenades."

"We don't have any grenades. The car is hot and no good outside the hills. You get two MP5s and an AK."

Besides being too big for me to conceal, an AK would leave me no bartering room for a small pistol that I could attempt to smuggle toward the Handler. I performed a quick function check on two of the MP5s, manipulating the fire selector and trigger in sequence to ensure they worked before slinging them over my shoulder, barrel down.

I spotted a Remington 870 breacher: a shortened, compact 12-gauge pump shotgun with a tactical sling.

It had certainly been a door-blasting tool for a police team, though I wasn't about to ask if it had been purchased from a corrupt cop or taken off a dead one. Appallingly short, it had no stock beyond the handgrip and no barrel beyond the magazine cap. Besides being easy for me to hide, it was everything the MP5 wasn't: dirt-cheap, difficult to control given its unmanageable recoil, and a leviathan of firepower. Its capacity was reduced from the full-sized version of the 870 in the interests of shortened size, but with three shells in the tube and one in the pipe, I felt good about its odds at close range.

I pointed to it. "This shotgun costs less than an AK. If I take this, I get a pistol too."

"That will take your hand off."

"That's my problem."

"The shotgun and a pistol. Then you're done." Enzo

spoke to one of his men, who began filling a backpack with loaded magazines and shotgun shells.

I hastily checked that the shotgun was in working order and approached the table of pistols. Beside a pile of uselessly rusted automatics and revolvers was a taser which, I thought with a wry smile, could be put to good use when Micah went on his next self-righteous tirade. I sorted through the pistols, finding a Taurus clone of the Beretta 92 we'd gotten from our driver yesterday. The sight of it gave me a sense of relief bordering on rapture—it was spotless, waiting to be found among a cast of trash pistols like an old friend.

Picking it up, I saw the tiny grip of an automatic pistol beneath it. I set the Taurus aside and extracted the miniature gun from the pile.

It was a Beretta 3032 Tomcat, a pistol so small that to fire its .32 ACP bullets—each less than an inch long—you'd only have room on the handgrip for your middle and index fingers. Impossibly small, and paper-thin in comparison to any other firearm in the dark armory, such a pistol could practically be tossed into your pocket and then lost while you fumbled for spare change without noticing it was gone.

I dropped the magazine and saw that it was fully loaded. Then I popped up the tip-up barrel to see the backing of a chambered round and received the business end of an AK-47 to my temple as a result.

I set the tiny .32 back down. At the time I didn't know how I could possibly get a gun close to the Handler, but if such a thing as a perfect assassination weapon hidden for me in Rio existed, then this was it. Knowing I was fated for death, and recalling my father's words the first time he handed me a pistol, I pointed to it.

"I'll take this one."

Enzo, in no mood for humor, looked and sounded impatient. "You plan on hunting rats?"

"Something like that."

Then Enzo's tone grew more serious and Gabriel's expression graver as he translated, "A shit heater like that only has one purpose, gringo."

"Again, that's my problem."

Enzo's voice lowered to a severe baritone. "Someone tried to kill me with that a few weeks ago. Taped it to his wrist, under his sleeve. My bodyguard—"

"*Filho da puta*," one of the men muttered.

"—my *late* bodyguard missed it during a pat down. The shot missed my head by a few inches."

I shook my head. "Bad marksmanship. Why was he trying to kill you?"

"I shot his brother."

"Seems a reasonable cause for revenge."

Enzo suddenly looked much older, his black eyes meeting mine with equal parts candor, pain, and some inexplicable third element. "I shot his brother three years before that."

"It took your shooter that long to find you?"

"No. He was waiting until he grew large enough to use the pistol. When he tried to kill me, he was nine years old. A born gangster, the kind I would have liked to hire, you see?" I nodded, and Enzo continued. "But his brother was a piece of shit. A rat. I killed him over some stupid girl. I cannot even remember her name now. You see the lesson there?"

"No."

"The problem I created was worse than the one I solved. Hunting rats can be a complex proposition. I almost died learning that lesson, and I have not forgotten it since. All because of that little pistol."

"Then you'll be glad to see it gone. Let me take it, *'al favor*, and I will tell my employer that you must be rewarded for your help."

Enzo eyed me warily. The events that drew me to him were what they were, and he had no choice but to regard me with suspicion, freeing me at best and killing me at worst.

Then he nodded his concession, and our business dealings were concluded.

* * *

Enzo and his crew walked us back to the front gate, where we were met head-on by two guards with a boy between them. The kid couldn't have been much older than seven, walking urgently with an envelope pinched in his tiny fist.

Our procession stopped abruptly as Enzo snatched the envelope and began ripping it open while exchanging Portuguese with the boy.

I looked to Gabriel for explanation.

"Courier," he said. "Police are still barricading the favela."

Enzo pulled a single sheet of paper from the envelope, and as he unfolded it I felt equal parts curiosity at its contents and a rabid desire to leave, with the balance focusing on the latter.

Enzo shouted, "*Espera aí!*"

Every gun was suddenly pointed at Gabriel and me.

I raised my hands non-threateningly. The pair of MP5s and the shotgun slung over my shoulder were empty, and most of the present company knew that—the backpack with the ammo and loaded .32 was still being toted by a guard.

Enzo examined the page, then my face, and back again.

"*No problema*," I said, resorting to my extremely limited Spanish and trying to keep my focus on Enzo's eyes. Gabriel and I were one word away from getting executed or worse, a mournful shift in fate after a negotiation that had yielded everything we hoped for except a radio.

Enzo rotated the paper so I could see it, pointing to a picture displayed in the middle of the page.

It was Micah, and beside his face was an image of Parvaneh.

Their expressions were focused, attention directed to something happening off-screen. I scanned the background of the photo and realized it was taken yesterday in Ribeiro's penthouse conference room.

My face and Gabriel's were absent from the page.

I dropped my hands. "I see all gringos look the same to you, *jefe*. But I'm ten years younger than the guy in that picture. And my translator here is a bitch, but he's nowhere near as hot as that *señorita*."

Gabriel translated, halting mid-sentence to glare at me when his mouth caught up with my description of him.

"Tell him," I said. Gabriel finished speaking, and Enzo's eyes didn't move from mine. Like most people whose lives had been a day-to-day process of survival, he'd learned to trust his intuition. And his intuition was telling him that I was lying as quickly as I could move my lips.

"Besides," I continued, "she's the reason I'm here in the first place."

Enzo's stare was fiery now, the consequences of

catching me in a lie growing along with his suspicion. "Explain."

"She slipped my ambush yesterday. Almost got killed chasing her here."

"This bounty is from my boss, the Master of Rocinha. But he sent it on behalf of the *big* boss."

"I warned you about my employer."

"Every mule thinks their middleman is God. You never said Ribeiro."

"Of course I didn't. Keep reading."

Enzo glanced at the paper, speaking succinctly as Gabriel said in English, "Cash reward for these two. Double if they're alive. And the pursuit team is to be helped in any way possible."

I gave a knowing nod and spoke with authority. "Good. That applies to me too."

But Enzo shook his head gravely. "This says I must comply with a team of men in uniform, with military equipment. You're some gringo off the street. Maybe you speak the truth or maybe you lie. But if you come back here again, I will kill you. That is the only warning you will get."

The gate was opened, and a shove sent me stumbling outside. Gabriel received the same farewell, tripping over his feet and falling to the ground before the metal doors slammed shut.

"Hey," I yelled. "What about our—"

The backpack with our ammo sailed over the wall, arcing above our heads as I raced in vain to catch it until it slammed into the ground, out of reach.

I grabbed it and hurriedly unzipped the back to begin loading our weapons.

"You can't be serious," Gabriel hissed. "Get out of the street with those guns."

I turned to see the favela around us filled with civilians.

* * *

In the streets of Rio that we'd traveled by Suburban yesterday, ducking into an alley for temporary isolation would have been a simple task. But the favela was no better for privacy than the center of Times Square. Instead, I followed Gabriel into the churning mass of bodies that flowed through the streets as people made their way through the slum.

I pulled my jacket over the pair of submachine guns and the breacher shotgun dangling from my shoulder, watching civilian eyes dart away from me as I did so. These people were no strangers to minding their own business, particularly when the alternative involved drawing the ire of someone with automatic weapons. Children scampered among the adult crowd, chasing each other and shouting in shrill voices. Skin colors ranged from every possible shade, with the balance falling amid coffee and cream. Most of the men and boys were shirtless, and those who didn't wear sandals simply walked barefoot.

Gabriel's scrawny form led me to a tight footpath between buildings, where we tucked ourselves into a small inlet stacked with milk crates as people passed behind us. For the moment, it was the closest we'd get to being hidden.

I dropped the backpack against the stucco wall and

knelt in front of it, loading and chambering an MP5. I slid two of the long, curved spare magazines into my belt.

"I can carry a gun," Gabriel said suddenly.

I loaded the shotgun with three shells from the back-pack, racking one into the chamber and slipping a fourth into the loading port. I asked, "Know how to use one?"

"Well—not really." His eyes darted from side to side with the admission, whether out of insecurity or general anxiety I couldn't tell.

"Then let me worry about shooting."

I slung the shotgun and MP5 beneath my wind-breaker. Then I found a discrete interior pocket in the backpack and inserted the .32 pistol inside, where it had the best chance of surviving a hasty pat down. I slipped the spare MP5 barrel-down inside the bag, zipping it shut into an oblong shape over the stock.

Behind me, Gabriel asked, "Why did you pick that little pistol? We could have used something bigger—"

"Five seconds ago you didn't know how to shoot. Now you're a pistol expert?"

"Well, no, but—"

"Then let me worry about the guns." I looked to the wall before us, its uneven brick surface covered in graffiti ranging from beautiful mosaic patterns to illegible scrawl. The centerpiece was a spray-painted image of a bull standing on two legs and holding a smoking gun. Beneath it a sprawl of graffiti read, *POLICIAIS SÃO MONSTROS.*

Eager to distract Gabriel from the pistol, I nodded to the image as I donned the backpack. "Does that mean what I think it does?"

"Police are monsters."

"If these people think the police are monsters, I

wonder what they're going to think about Ribeiro's kill team. Come on. Let's go find the other two."

Leaving the footpath, we proceeded along the side of a road descending a hill, where the buildings—if you could call them that—were a testament to decades of haphazard repair using sheet metal and slats of wood from shipping pallets.

As soon as Gabriel and I had set off for the local narco-mansion that morning, Micah had relocated Parvaneh to places unknown. His logic was sound, preventing her compromise in the not-unlikely event that Gabriel and I were caught and tortured into betraying their location. But this precaution had necessitated a corresponding link-up plan, and so instead of returning to a known point, we were to walk down a central market street until Micah signaled us.

Gabriel appeared at ease among the people, but my senses were on high alert. While we could meld into the crowd, there was no escaping the stationary watchers sitting on every flat surface and looking out from windows and balconies overhead. Our only security was to keep our heads down and continue moving. I whipped my head sideways at the sudden whooping of adolescent boys, seeing them inside an open doorway playing a video game.

"Start talking," Gabriel said. "Look casual."

"All right. You did good back there."

"Is that your apology for threatening to shoot me in the car last night?"

I ducked out of the way of two children racing past, shrieking as they chased each other. "No."

"You may be the hired gun, David, but I've got many years of service to the Organization."

"Don't really care."

We crossed into a colorful, bustling marketplace. The architectural chaos around us succumbed to orderly merchandise from clothes to fruit stacked and lined as neatly as one could find anywhere in the world. Clothes, produce, and electronics, along with their vendors, were shaded by bed sheets strung overhead across the road. I was relieved to spot bottled water. My thirst was a cruel repetition after the African desert, and I felt a compulsion to stock up as much as we could.

I reached into my sock and pulled a few spare bills I'd stashed. "Let's pick up some food and water."

He took the money, saying nothing before approaching a vendor.

I stopped at a row of foldout tables with precisely stacked pyramids of oranges, apples, bananas, and vegetables. Gabriel did the buying, unzipping the bag on my back and placing his purchases inside. My eyes fell upon a table loaded with piles of raw fish. The gray bodies were heaped atop one another in a collective mound of death, though not motionless—dark flies clustered around agape mouths and lifeless eyes emerged from the pile in every direction.

I looked over my shoulder at Gabriel, who was placing his purchases beside the weapon in my bag. "Zip it up. We're done."

We continued walking through the crowd, heading downhill past a few tables of old men playing dominoes. Micah shouldn't be much farther ahead, I thought, trying to listen for the call of his voice guiding us toward his new refuge. Instead, I heard a low drumming sound over the noise of the crowd, so faint at first I thought it must have been wishful thinking. Then it grew louder, erasing any doubt in my mind—a helicopter was skimming the favela to our front.

"You hear that?" I said excitedly. "The Outfit helicopter is flying search patterns. If it gets close enough, we can—"

Gabriel cut me off. "I looked over your file before you got down here. We pulled it as soon as we found out who we were waiting for."

My file. Of course the entire delegation would have read it by now: even Sage, my attractive redheaded flight attendant onboard the Handler's jet, had seen it before picking me up from the Complex.

I said, "And I'll bet you're about to tell me every profound deduction you've made on my worth as a human being."

"You didn't report any Latin American countries on your prior travel."

We bypassed a hill of bloated canvas sacks leaning against a wall. "That's because I've never been there before."

"No, you've been to the Dominican Republic. Not the tourist areas, either."

It was getting harder to act normal as we continued walking. My short stay in that country had bridged the gap between my time with Boss's team and the Outfit, and it had no explanation besides being a criminal exile that I had to keep secret at all costs.

"That's fascinating, because I've never visited. Tell me more."

"Back there during the arms buy. You were trying to say please, but you said *'al favor.'*"

The sound of the helicopter faded. "So?"

"That's short for *haz al favor.* Spanish, but a very specific dialect."

"Might have picked it up from someone in the Army."

"I don't think so, David. My guess is you spent time in the rough areas of the southern Dominican, probably Barahona Province. There are some fugitive communities in that area. It would be of great interest to the Handler if you lied about having been there."

"You're reading too far into this."

"Maybe. I think I'll report you anyway, just to be safe. The Organization comes first in all things."

"How dutiful of you. Report whatever you want because—"

A burst of automatic gunfire came from above and behind us.

The first sound of the attack wasn't the gunshots themselves; someone was firing supersonic rounds from a suppressed weapon. As a result, all we heard was a cracking whip of bullets breaking the sound barrier as they sliced through the favela's dank air and laced into human flesh. A woman beside us flung her legs upward as if she'd slipped on an oil spot, and a grizzled man moving the opposite direction dropped to his knees.

Gabriel took a stuttering step, confused, his lack of survival instinct maddening to me as I grabbed him and hurled him behind the nearest cover.

That cover happened to be a few short stacks of car tires not nearly big enough to hide behind, but all we had was a wall of collapsed civilians between the shooter and us. Gabriel hit the street hard and I dove atop him a moment later, desperately claiming what little real estate there was to occupy.

The favela residents were no strangers to gunfire—the initial scream of a woman could be heard, perhaps, but it was then followed by the silent, orderly scuffle of a tremendous mass of people to indoor locations of relative safety. There was no trampling the fallen, no endless shrieks of despair. Instead the crowds fled with a sobriety forged through frequent exposure to violence.

I got to my knees and readied the MP5 against my shoulder, then leaned out from the side of the tires with my sights up.

A *brrap* of bullets hit the tires to my front, the vibration of the impacting rounds reverberating against me as a heaving shudder in the rubber. Based on terrain, the shooter couldn't be more than a hundred meters away.

The walls around us were a staggered, swirling mass of roof atop roof, marred in all directions by a thousand black spider eyes of windows. Even if I miraculously identified the shooter at a millisecond's glance, I had no chance of effectively returning fire.

Gabriel looked at me, his expression betraying a terrified search for reassurance in my face and finding none. "What do we do?"

Our situation was worse than he realized—the tires provided temporary reprieve from being shot, but our assailant didn't care if he killed us. The suppressed gunfire meant he was one of the three men we had seen extinguishing our rescue signal last night, and he was now pinning us down after a chance sighting. We would have been better off hearing multiple shooters: a single gunman meant the other two men were maneuvering in to finish us off.

I inhaled the toxic smell of burning rubber as bullets smoldered inside the tires and looked for our options, however bleak.

The wall behind us had no immediate door in sight, and the nearest alley to the right was set far into the now-abandoned marketplace. To our left was a staircase descending the hill, but to reach it required a ten-foot sprint across open ground.

"See that staircase to our left?" I asked. "Wait for me to distract the shooter and then run there faster than you ever have in your life. I won't be able to buy you much time."

Sliding to the opposite side of the tire pile, I exposed my MP5 barrel as if by accident. Another hailstorm of rounds came racing into the tires, and by the time I recoiled and told Gabriel to move, he was already sprinting away.

The impact of bullets spread along the wall behind his racing figure, the spray of fire ending abruptly before he vanished down the stairs.

The shooter was either reloading or baiting me to move, and I didn't wait to find out if it was the latter. I instinctively flung myself toward the stairs, falling short and slamming on my side before rolling over the edge.

A tumbling fall took me halfway down before I clipped the legs of Gabriel, who, between revolutions, I vaguely saw leaping down the steps. Our impact sent him sprawling behind me. The weapon inside the backpack slammed against my spine as the MP5 and shotgun at my side pinned against my rattling ribs.

We crashed to a flat landing in the staircase, and before Gabriel recovered his wits I grabbed his shirt and threw him into a gap between buildings. Then I followed him down the tight alley in the hopes our pursuers would assume we had continued down the stairs. Civilians in the alley vanished into the walls to either side like tiny fish darting into crevices of coral. The sound of gunplay on the street above hadn't caused them to hide, but the appearance of two bleeding and desperate men drawing hunters their way surely did.

Oblivious to the gunfire, a horse comprised of little more than skin and bone chewed on the contents of a filth-coated trash bin in the alley. We ran around it, cutting down a cobblestone footpath and around another corner before I heard the sounds of men running and shouting to one another.

I pulled Gabriel into a tight wall inlet amid the reeking stench of urine, pointing my MP5 at the corner to our front. The sounds of our pursuers seemed to be moving downhill behind us, following the stairs to lower ground as I'd hoped.

Once I could no longer hear them, I turned to face Gabriel.

He was breathing hard, panicking, his hand clasping the back of his scalp and coming away bloody. He looked to me for guidance, a child judging the severity of their fall by the reaction of the nearest adult.

"Better than getting shot," I whispered. "Come on, we need to make our way back to the market street."

"No! We can't go back."

"They won't expect it. And—"

"I won't go. I can't."

"All you have to do is follow me. Okay? If we don't link up with Micah we're dead anyway."

"I can hide here."

"Think about it. No one's sending a helicopter for either of us once Parvaneh makes it out. We've got to head back."

I turned and left our hiding spot before he had time to overthink our situation, hoping that my departure would cause him to blindly follow me.

Glancing over my shoulder, I saw that it had. He shuffled behind me, his poise an awkward, fearful scatter as he anticipated further gunshots.

I took a circuitous route back toward the link-up road, proceeding with measured caution. The ease with which I could lose orientation in the favela, and the death sentence that represented, made me hyperalert. I looked up to the intersecting buildings looming over us in every direction, our surroundings bursting with makeshift drainage systems, rubble, bicycles, laundry drying on clotheslines and windowsills. I could hear the murmur of adult voices mingled with the crying of babies all around, but the outdoor spaces were remarkably abandoned as the population collectively waited out the shooting.

We continued threading through gaps in the labyrinth, making steady progress before a stationary shadow at the end of an alley suddenly shifted.

We broke into a run as the first bullets cracked through the air. Gabriel matched my dead sprint as I desperately tried to maintain my bearings. If the kill team was smart enough to fake their departure while leaving a shooter behind to wait us out, the other members wouldn't be long in reinforcing him.

I turned one corner, then two, before finding a tight opening between buildings where gravity could once again work in our favor: a narrow channel was covered in several feet of trash sloping steeply downhill.

Flinging myself into it without a second thought, I scrambled down the shifting landscape beneath me, skidding over slimy plastic bags and moldy cloth atop a decaying sludge, the reeking stench only slightly more bearable than the kill team that followed behind us.

After fifty feet of a tumbling crawl downhill, I grabbed

the corner of a wall and pulled myself into an adjoining footpath before looking up the way I had come.

Gabriel was gone.

Had he missed my turn into the channel? It was possible, though more likely he'd abandoned me, convinced his chances of survival were greater on his own.

I heard another burst of gunfire somewhere above, the unmistakable sonic crack of bullets echoing through the slum's corridors. Readying the MP5, I prepared to go back for him. The thought of doing otherwise was revolting on a primal level, whether or not he was going to expose my time in the Dominican Republic. I'd been ready to punch him in the face minutes earlier, but the appearance of a worse external threat had turned Gabriel into a brother by circumstance.

But I had resources that Parvaneh needed—the food and water, weapons, and, most importantly, information. She and Micah didn't realize that flyers bearing their faces were being distributed to every armed gang in the favela, didn't know that Ribeiro had definitively placed a bounty for their kill or capture. Instead they were huddled in some crevice or another, possessing a single pistol with a few remaining rounds, waiting for an Outfit invasion once night fell. And the carnage of civilians on the market street was nothing in light of what would transpire if that event occurred as planned.

* * *

I continued moving down the footpath and toward the market road as silently as I could, tucking the slung MP5 under my jacket. A few faces began to appear in windows and doorways around me, assessing the safety of their surroundings before they spilled back into the slum's corridors. As I finally made out the market road to my front, I heard Micah's harsh whisper.

"David."

I turned toward the noise. A primitive, muddy concrete staircase ascended and twisted sideways into an opening at the side of a wall made of square red bricks. At the top, a cat watched me from a dark window before vanishing inside.

Micah's voice again.

"David."

Kneeling down, I saw the vague outline of his face in the shadows beneath the exposed stairs. I ducked down into the space and out of view to the alley behind me. Micah crawled forward to make room for two new occupants before he stopped and turned, waiting for Gabriel to enter and realizing he had been lost to us.

He whispered, "Radio?"

I gave a slight shake of my head, drawing back a side of my jacket to reveal the MP5 and shotgun. Without a word, he spun and crawled on all fours into a gap in the cinderblocks behind him.

I followed him through a muddy shaft between buildings, shuffling through the soggy slime of earth eternally protected from the light of day. The path led into a small crevice lit by shafts of sunlight permeating through gaps in the structures around it.

Seated there, with beams of yellow light blazing stripes across her figure, was Parvaneh.

She looked strangely comfortable in that space, legs drawn up under her arms like she was sitting around a campfire. Her dark hair was neatly parted, descending on either side of her face. Even the dried mud on her body seemed dignified evidence of an adventurous nature, as if she were royalty who had transcended mortal toil and nonetheless chosen to enter the wilderness.

Her jade green eyes creased in disappointment, bringing me back to the sordid reality that I had returned alone.

"He made it out of the initial ambush," I said before she could ask. "We ran, and he was right behind me. I took a turn, and he didn't." I momentarily considered adding the sound of final gunshots that I'd heard and decided to omit this to spare her what little hurt I could. "He could still be evading. If anyone can talk their way through the favela, it's him."

"What'd you get?" Micah asked.

"They didn't have radios or grenades." I took the backpack off my shoulder, snatching it away as Micah reached for it. "I snagged two MP5s and a breacher shotgun."

"I asked you for an AR pistol. They didn't have any?"

"Christ, Micah. You want guns? I went into a drug den and got you guns. If they had AR pistols you'd be holding one right now." I laid out the contents of my bag, starting with the food and water and stopping before I reached the .32 pistol.

Parvaneh watched me with an unwavering focus. "Was it the same men who extinguished our signal fires last night?"

"Definitely."

Micah checked that the other MP5 was loaded before slinging it across his chest. "We need to be certain."

"Suppressed weapons and wildly effective use of fire and maneuver. It was them."

Parvaneh wasn't convinced. "This favela is controlled

by drug traffickers. How can three men pursue us freely while we have to hide?"

I picked up a bottle of water and offered it to her. She didn't accept it.

"They're protected," I said.

"Not by our employer," Micah interjected. "His is the only protection that matters."

"This isn't his turf."

"Everywhere is his 'turf.' Who's protecting them?"

I set the water bottle down and wiped a slick of mud off my pants. "Ribeiro."

Parvaneh smiled as if coaxing a child to tell the truth. "There are consequences to what you say, David. You must be certain before making accusations like this."

"A courier arrived when I was leaving the trafficker's house. He brought orders that the kill team isn't to be interfered with. Pictures of you and Micah inside the conference room yesterday, a bounty for you both—"

"*Senhor* Ribeiro could be trying to recover us."

"—double if you're delivered alive."

Micah's eyes cut to Parvaneh. Her smile remained, though the rest of her face assumed a pallor of fury.

"I'm going to crucify him," she said.

Micah spoke harshly. "You're certain about everything you just said?"

"The drug boss we met was going to kill us. I convinced him I was working for Ribeiro too, that I chased her into the favela."

"He bought that?"

"Not really, but he wasn't about to risk being wrong. They don't know who the Handler is, but they're scared shitless of Ribeiro."

Parvaneh was unmoved. "They'll know who the Handler is very, very soon."

My mind seamlessly crossed from a recollection of Karma being killed beside me to waking up strapped to the electric chair, the wet sponge and leather straps tight against my body as the Handler toyed with the switch. I cleared my throat, carefully wording my next statement. "I think it's time we considered the possibility that the Handler is working with Ribeiro to kill us."

Micah actually laughed. It was the first indication yet that he possessed a sense of humor, and he displayed it with the awkwardness of a newborn calf learning to walk for the first time. "Don't be ridiculous."

I said, "Laughter doesn't suit you, Micah. And the Handler was prepared to execute me at my meeting with him—that much I'm certain of. But he ordered me to meet his delegation in Brazil instead."

Parvaneh waved a hand at me, her mind elsewhere. "He's not colluding with Ribeiro. That's the one thing about this situation I can tell you with total certainty."

I watched her closely. "Think, Parvaneh. You had to leave a trained bodyguard behind to take me along. He wants me dead. He had the chance to kill two birds with one stone by sending me here, and he took it."

"He sent you here," Parvaneh said bluntly, "because beneath his façade of genius lurks a superstitious madman."

Micah suffered a barely contained explosion.

"That *superstition*," he spat, "has saved his family's legacy and their place at the head of the Organization more than once. And in a long line of great men to occupy the position he now holds, he is universally regarded as the greatest. There have been many Handlers, but he is the One." The last word caught in his throat as he regained himself, eyes flicking toward me in a self-conscious realization that came too late. "Ma'am."

Parvaneh didn't seem to mind his breach of professional courtesy. She reached to the ground and procured a bruised apple from the pile of food. "Every generation has said that about their leader. Ours is another raving murderous bastard just like the rest."

"You stand alone, ma'am."

She took a bite, chewing slowly before swallowing, as if using the pause to make sure she wanted to say her next words. "If I stand alone, it's because those who agree with me are kept silent by fear. And for good reason."

"He can't afford to take chances. The Organization comes first in all things."

Parvaneh said nothing. She knew Micah harbored a fanaticism that couldn't be reasoned with, and rather than try further she retreated into silence.

Seeing the divide between them, I stepped into the gap.

"You two need to tell me why I'm here."

"False counsel," Parvaneh said at once.

Micah corrected her. "Counsel that has been right in the past, and without which our leader wouldn't have claim to the throne he now holds."

"Blind luck," she replied.

"The Organization owes its very existence to that luck."

"Jesus," I blurted, "stop speaking in riddles. I got off a plane from Africa and ended up in this shithole a week later, and everyone knows why but me. For once, can somebody just tell me what in the fuck you're talking about. In plain English."

Parvaneh smiled, my frustration providing a rare moment of amusement in the midst of her official duties. "You know better than we do, David. The Silver Widow."

I looked at her blankly. "What about her?"

"After meeting you, she delivered a prophecy that you would save my life. And since the Handler is the one person left who listens to prophecy, he believes that without you, I'm as good as dead."

In a flash, I understood it all.

That's why the young Somali woman separated Caspian and me upon our arrival to her hideout, summoning only me to meet her. She wanted the Handler dead and had assumed the Silver Widow's identity before receiving us. Gaining my complicity, she intervened on my behalf with a false prophecy. If I hadn't followed her advice and confirmed that she didn't speak or remove her mask, the prophecy would be dismissed, and I'd have died in the Handler's chair—before my first sunset in America, just as she'd said.

You do not grasp the danger you are in.

That's why she said we had only a few years, and not a decade, before the Handler realized the truth. The Silver Widow, the *real* Silver Widow, was aged to muteness. A false prophecy was only as good as the belief that it had come from her, and she was at best a few years from death. The young woman insisted she would help me, but only if I lied about my meeting with her. That's what she meant—if I didn't convince the Handler that I'd met with the Silver Widow, he'd have no reason to keep me alive.

That's why he had strapped me to the electric chair and interrogated me about her. The possibility of my collusion with the Indian was a distant second to his true priority of protecting his envoy.

Parvaneh spoke. "So quiet all of a sudden, David. What's the matter, it doesn't make any more sense to you than it does to me?"

"No. That...can't be right."

"It shouldn't be right. But it is."

"If he truly believes I'm going to save you, why did he treat me like a death-row inmate during our meeting?"

"Part of his routine for honoring first-time visitors. In his mind, everyone is trying to kill him."

My mind was set aflame with the words *first-time visitors*. So, there was a chance I'd undergo less scrutiny on my return. With a man like the Handler, a chance was all I'd ever get—and if I was lucky, all I'd need.

"What about putting me in the electric chair? Is that part of his routine too?"

Micah replied before Parvaneh could. "More of a lie detector. You must have said at least one truthful thing to be here now."

Parvaneh flinched but continued, "Because the Handler listens to this prophetic nonsense, my entire delegation was halted until you could arrive. And since I was ordered to keep you at my side, I now have one world-class bodyguard here instead of two."

"With me," I said, "one is all you need. And while Micah may not be world-class *per se*, he's not bad as a sidekick—"

Micah flexed his hands into fists and cut me off. "She's talking about me."

Parvaneh giggled, and the way Micah's face swung toward her in response made it apparent he feared losing control.

Aside from the fact that I enjoyed pissing him off, Parvaneh represented the greatest ally I could have. If the

Handler considered her important enough to keep me alive to save her, then earning her favor was my best chance of smuggling the .32 pistol close enough to him to use it.

Micah looked to Parvaneh and said, "Every decision that seemed lunacy at the time has turned out to have been made with a foresight rivaling omnipotence. We shouldn't be questioning the One. Especially not in front of an outsider."

She replied, "That's the problem, Micah. No one questions him, and then when he obeys the ranting of a leprous old hag, we assume it must be a mark of psychic genius."

I took a breath. "We need to discuss our options."

Micah bristled with superiority. "There are no options. You tried to get a radio. You failed. We hide here until the Outfit invades tonight, and that's final."

"My picture wasn't on the bounty."

"And if Gabriel were still here to translate, that might mean something. But you didn't bring him back."

"Take a break from playing armchair quarterback, just for a minute. You must have heard the Outfit helicopter flying search patterns over us. I can signal it and get them to drop off a team of shooters."

"Ribeiro's kill team will find you long before that point."

"Even better. If I kill them, I get a radio and bring it back. You can raise the Outfit on their emergency frequency, and the helicopter comes to us."

He snorted. "A bald twenty-year-old kid—"

"Twenty-five. And I had salon-quality hair until this brilliant visionary you keep breathlessly speaking of hooked me up to a fucking electric chair."

Another grin from Parvaneh before Micah shot back, "You're not going to prevail over three trained and equipped operators. Whoever they are, they've seen worse than you."

"No, they haven't. And I'm willing to fight to the death for Parvaneh just like you are."

"You're willing to fight to the death for anything. That's not loyalty, it's lunacy. Don't think for a minute that we didn't read every word of your file before you arrived."

"Yeah, I keep hearing that. Apparently the only one not to read the fucking thing was me."

"Major depressive disorder with suicidal ideation. Pronounced posttraumatic stress. And a history of alcoholism."

"Alcoholism? Would an alcoholic be sober for"—I glanced at my watch—"almost forty-eight hours?"

"David," Parvaneh said, her hint of a smile fading, "Micah's right. There's no way you'll win in a three-on-one engagement."

"Every man on that kill team is telling themselves the same thing. And after how they reacted during that last gunfight, I can guarantee they'll pursue once they see me. This time I'm alone, and I can buttonhook and find a hiding place."

Parvaneh said, "You'll be killed in seconds."

"So what if I am?" I looked at her emphatically, exploiting her lack of immediate refusal to drive my point. "The Handler almost killed me once; he's certainly going to finish the job once he realizes he's an asshole for listening to some old crone reading chicken bones in the desert. I'm supposed to save your life? Then let me go save your life."

Micah summoned her attention with an outstretched

palm. "If he leaves, I have to relocate you and establish a new link-up plan in case he's compromised. That endangers you and gains us nothing."

"Hiding gains us nothing," I countered. "She's not safer the longer she stays here. If the kill team captured Gabriel alive, then he's already told them our link-up plan. That puts them closer to her than they were before. And let's not pretend we can't prevent innocent deaths by calling the helicopter."

"We can't," Micah said flatly.

"You may not have just watched a bunch of civilians get mowed down by Ribeiro's kill team, but I did. And that was just one of their guys shooting at Gabriel and me. What happens when the entire Outfit invades? Ribeiro will send reinforcements, and the drug traffickers will either fight for him or try to defend their turf. Now we're talking a three-way crossfire in the most densely populated place in the country. How many more innocent people need to be murdered because you want to hide?"

Parvaneh's face went cold.

Micah observed her reaction and redoubled his efforts. "The Organization comes first in all things. We will do whatever has the best chance of returning you safely, and right now that is to wait—"

Parvaneh brought her hands swiftly together, steepling her fingertips in front of her face. "Both of you will do whatever I order."

Micah's body language shifted to subservience at once —face lowered, hands settling in his lap. I stayed frozen, waiting for her to speak again.

"I will not have further civilian blood on my hands while we have an option to prevent it. If David leaves, he will either die, bring back a radio, or signal the helicopter himself. Two out of those three will save the lives of people endangered by my presence here. My decision is final."

A beat of silence, her words hanging in the air between us.

As I opened my mouth to respond, Micah spoke.

"Langley has already lost one parent, ma'am."

Parvaneh's face turned to nearly the same mask of rage that it had with the evidence of Ribeiro's betrayal. I glanced to the engagement ring on her hand, saw her watching me, and looked away.

Her next words were spoken with a measured cadence. "I need no reminders about what happened to her father. If David dies, that is on my shoulders and not yours. But he chose to serve. I will not have innocents needlessly lose their lives because of my refusal to assume risk."

Micah's gaze fell to the dirt, but I could see his shoulders rising and falling with quickened breath. He had lost some strategic game whose intent I didn't understand, but the magnitude of this failure seemed clear enough to him.

Parvaneh reached out and clasped my hand in hers, her palms soft and her eyes on mine with an intense stare.

"I order you to summon my rescue before nightfall. The only failure is in death."

I thought back to Micah and Gabriel's response to her order yesterday. "I hear and I obey."

Micah watched me with a grim expression, saying nothing.

5

I set off uphill in the afternoon light, the MP5 and breacher shotgun slung under my jacket. After splitting the ammunition with Micah, I had 120 9mm rounds and a handful of buckshot to eliminate a three-man team if I couldn't signal the helicopter first. It wasn't a lot of ammo under normal circumstances, but I wouldn't find myself in a protracted firefight. I'd either get the drop on Ribeiro's kill team, hit them before they realized what was happening, and finish them off together, or I'd be dead long before I fired my last bullet.

My eyes darted to windows, rooftops, spider holes, and staircases layered in all directions. The entire mass of shanties rose ever higher in a human morass through which I moved, never certain that I wasn't being watched and always knowing that I was being hunted. The sensation was particularly unsettling given that I had come under fire in the same setting a few hours earlier. The undercurrent of adrenaline humming in my veins, normally my greatest incentive, was now rendered a painful reminder of the horrifying and very real possibility of civilian deaths due to my actions.

And shockingly, the very same people who had made their orderly flight indoors when Gabriel and I were ambushed had now returned to the streets and sidewalks, manning their market stands and making their way to and from parts unknown. There were fewer of them than there had been that morning, and though the sparse crowds seemed particularly free from small children chasing each other, they had returned nonetheless.

The best protection I could give them was to move quickly, reducing their exposure time to danger by virtue of my presence. Without Gabriel to translate, I had little alternative. As a non-Portuguese-speaking gringo setting off against three trained killers, my odds couldn't have been much worse. Throw in the likelihood of a chance encounter with an armed trafficker, and I'd be lucky to last ten minutes.

Yet by all accounts, setting off on my own was the smartest move I could make.

If my current survival owed itself to a false prophecy, then it wouldn't last for long. But if I could singlehandedly initiate Parvaneh's rescue, I stood a chance of endearing myself to her. She was important enough to bypass routine security searches, and out of everyone surrounding the Handler—his pilots, Sage, the men who'd delivered me to his building, and certainly Racegun —Parvaneh was the only one who seemed able to help me get close to him, inadvertently or not.

Even with the chance association with her and the .32 I'd been able to scoop, my odds of success were almost nonexistent. But against the concentric and obsessive levels of security I faced upon returning to the Handler's compound, they were the best I'd ever get.

I heard the unmistakable echo of helicopter blades drumming toward me from the east. Without a second of hesitation, I ran toward a three-story structure whose ground comprised a storefront and desperately called to the vendors inside.

"Roof," I said, pointing to the sky. "Up."

They gestured to one corner, where I found a stairwell wrapping crudely around the side of the building. Running up its dirty, exposed stairs, I found the roof to be little more than a few sheets of thin corrugated iron laid over walls. I cautiously tested the surface with my foot, and the slapdash arrangement of metal bowed under my weight, nearly collapsing with me on top of it. I found the longest continuous sheet of metal and followed it, threading my way to a more stable balcony on the far side. Once I reached it, I only had to pull myself atop a platform holding two plastic water tanks to catch my first visual of the aircraft.

It was unmistakably the Outfit helicopter that I had seen atop the freighter after my arrival to Rio, now flying perhaps a quarter mile distant. It hammered across the sky at an altitude of three hundred feet over the multicolored matrix below. I watched its shadow coast across a sea of roofs sprouting satellite dishes, their broken-down buildings camouflaged by decades of graffiti. The helo was grazing up the hill in low switchbacks, searching for a signal from its lost delegation amidst the maze.

"*Oye porra*," a young male voice called behind me. "*Venha aqui.*"

I turned to see the voice had come from a youth in his early teens at best, standing on the far side of the roof. A constellation of boys reached the top of the stairs behind him and spread out to his sides. Many of them dangled automatic pistols from their hands, the oldest of the group bearing gold jewelry and designer sneakers.

Above the burning tingle of panic, I reminded myself that the surest way to get shot was to show fear. Maintaining the same calm assurance that I'd addressed Enzo with, I called back, "English?"

"*Não fode, maluco.*"

There were six, standing close enough together for me to mow them down like dry grass with the four shells of buckshot in my shotgun.

He pointed to the weapons under my jacket. "*Porque que tu ta armado?*"

I heard a noise behind me and glanced over my shoulder. Another group of boys now blocked the way I'd come, a few of them pointing sideways pistols at me and, therefore, at their comrades as well.

Behind them, the helicopter worked its way closer.

The boys were unconcerned about the aircraft, having a short lifetime of experience to tell them that threats didn't come from the sky in their urban rainforest. If the Complex operators spotted me, the helo doors would slide open, and I'd need only hit the deck before the gang was killed outright or sent scattering from an opening salvo of precision fire.

I had to buy myself one minute, maybe less. "Enzo," I said confidently. "Enzo. ADA."

I waited for the reverence of this name to quell the immediate physical danger. Instead it provoked a low chant from the boys, rising in pitch with the taunting intonation of a schoolyard challenge. The group's attention shifted at once to the kid who'd addressed me, waiting for his reaction with a "what you gonna do about it" antic-ipation.

"*O Enzo que sa foda*," he shouted with sneering contempt, before breaking out into a long, chattering rant in Portuguese that was intended, I supposed, for the benefit of his associates.

A rival gang.

"Ribeiro!" I called in desperation. "My boss is *Senhor* Ribeiro."

This evoked a louder burst of laughter—of course it did. I could barely talk my way out of execution when I had Gabriel translating for me. Without him, I was fucked. Nothing was more dangerous right now than a group of kids who were armed, thought themselves invin-cible, and were possibly on drugs. They probably couldn't hit a man-sized target with a handgun unless they were close enough to touch it anyway, but at that range and in those numbers, they wouldn't have to. I could exploit their poor marksmanship with lateral movement, but that meant a blind leap that was becoming more likely with each passing second.

Instead I hoped for the helicopter to drown out his voice, for its descending rotor wash to whip a tornado of sand as the shooters onboard opened fire, for the Handler's wrath to descend like the hand of God to save me. But its noise grew distant as the aircraft cut a path in the wrong direction, swinging west as the ringleader's pistol raised toward me, the black pit of the barrel staring at my face.

More barrels pointed in my direction, all exits blocked by the boys holding them.

I was already a target; now I had seconds to become a moving one.

Taking two running steps sideways, I leapt over the blind edge and off the roof.

A pair of booming gunshots followed, but my attention shifted to the immediate physical danger of the void opening beneath me. My stomach lurched into my throat. I tried to bring my feet and knees together to keep my bones intact, but there was no time. Ten vertical feet went by in a flash, and my feet slammed into a flat roof outcropping.

I felt a searing, burning pain in my right knee upon impact. Instead of becoming stationary and evaluating my next move, I fell sprawling off the side as my leg buckled.

As I fell through a bed sheet strung over the street, my vision became a cocoon of white. A split second later, I crashed into a table below it.

The table flipped sideways under my weight and I rolled to the ground.

As I flung the table off me, my first view at street level revealed a mass of people scattering with only slightly less urgency than I felt, fleeing with a practiced efficiency from the sound of more gunshots.

I fought my way upward and took off in a sprint for the far side of the street, my run an awkward accommodation of a suddenly resistant right knee. A splattering of bullet impacts cracked off the building in front of me just before I kicked open the nearest door and flung myself into a home.

I glanced back the way I had come but regretted doing so at once.

It looked like I was watching a film in fast-forward. The child gangsters bounded down the stairs to street level, hurdling obstacles and snaking between fleeing bystanders at lightning speed.

They'd be upon me in seconds no matter what I did, probably in far greater numbers if I killed one of them. I pulled the MP5 from beneath my jacket, raising it to fire a few rounds out the doorway to stall them and continue my escape.

As I raised the stock to my shoulder, the lead boy fell mid-stride as he raced across the street. It looked as if he'd tripped until the bloody puddle appeared beneath him.

The whistling howl of suppressed gunshots flew in from somewhere down the street, and a few boys reacted by returning fire to my left. They fell where they took their last stand, screams of pain silenced by kill shots as the rest of the child gang reversed course and faded into the shantytown behind them.

Ribeiro's kill team wasn't interested in seeing me killed by gangbangers—they wanted me alive and were intervening to keep me that way. Parvaneh was their real prize, and they'd use me to find her however they could.

I turned and plunged deeper into the home, passing through a curtain separating a living room attached to a half-kitchen. Searching desperately for an ambush position, I saw a single loveseat, a bathroom the size of a phone booth concealed behind a half-open sheet, and, behind a short counter, a waist-high cabinet big enough for me to squeeze into.

Without time to second-guess my decision, I threw open the home's far door, leaving it ajar to reveal the alleyway beyond as if I'd continued running. Then I opened the cabinet, finding a sparse collection of what few cooking pots and pans the occupants owned. Noisily shoving them aside to make room for myself, I ducked inside the cabinet.

I arranged the MP5 over my chest and pulled the

doors almost completely shut behind me, leaving a crack so I could see into the kitchen.

Then I placed my foot against one door so I could kick it open and settled the breacher shotgun into my grasp with its barrel angled forward.

The kill team probably wore body armor. That was no problem—in that event, the pelvis was an often-over-looked target. I'd score mobility kills outright, and even if they were able to return fire from the floor, they wouldn't be able to do so for long. Femoral arteries converged at this fragile junction of the human structure, and the effects of a load of 12-gauge buckshot searing into it from behind at close range would quickly be fatal.

A sudden thumping of footsteps in the room behind me signaled the arrival of my first pursuer. I tried to quiet my breathing, palms settling on the worn synthetic shotgun grip. The footsteps drew closer toward the kitchen until a shadow fell across the floor, and I drew a final breath and held it as a figure crossed in front of me.

It was a young girl.

I burst out of the cabinet as her terrified eyes found me, my shotgun lowered and a finger pressed to my lips to indicate silence.

I pointed to the door behind us. Lacking sufficient Portuguese vocabulary, I reverted to the graffiti I had seen in the alley with Gabriel. "Monsters. *Monstros.*"

She covered her throat with a tiny hand and replied shakily, "*Monstros?*"

"Yes, yes. *Monstros.* Go," I told her, gesturing to the far door. "Run."

But she was riveted with fear, even as a renewed flurry of screams from the street indicated the kill team's arrival.

I grabbed her with one hand and yanked her into the

cabinet with me, pulling the doors closed just as more footsteps sounded from the room behind us. Placing a hand over her mouth, I tensed the other on the shotgun grip as the kill team flooded into the kitchen.

Their entry was quiet, their movements a graceful, unscripted free-flow dance of room clearing. Short-whip radio antennas protruded from plate carriers that held it all: water supply, grenades, ammunition, medical supplies, and, most importantly, radios. Everything I needed and more to rescue Parvaneh, mine for the taking save the unexpected intrusion of the girl who had returned home a minute too soon.

The dark shapes flowed past, sweeping suppressed M4 assault rifles over the space as they headed for the back door that I had deliberately left ajar. But as the three men slipped into the alley, a fourth man entered the kitchen.

Then a fifth.

A hot flood of tears joined the little girl's breath on my hand as I waited for the kill team to pass, mentally cursing my unexpected odds. Three against one was bad, and five against one far worse than I was equipped to deal with even if the girl hadn't shown up. In the seconds it would take me to open fire on the first three, two others would be burning me down.

The last man stopped suddenly, rotating sideways as if he'd detected something out of place.

My heart rate rocketed as I watched him through the crack between the doors, strangely expecting his face to be the Handler's. Time suspended its march forward as the man stood completely motionless, half-looking in my direction as he detected something he couldn't explain. The terror of the moment was amplified as I gained a clear view of his profile and indisputably recognized him.

It was Agustin, the bearded man who had gazed across the Rio landscape with me as he contemplated the statue of Christ the Redeemer.

I could have gotten the jump on him, I knew—could have sent a load of buckshot his way as my shotgun blast beat the response of any return fire. But with four other teammates, it would be the last thing I'd ever do.

And the girl in my grasp would certainly be caught in the crossfire.

I waited in silence as Agustin swiftly turned and slipped out the back door, following the first four into the alleyway. I remained still, waiting to be sure they were gone.

A long minute passed before the girl's body tensed and she threw my hands off her, tumbling out of the cabinet.

I unfolded myself behind her as she turned to boldly face me.

Then I peeled a yellow bill from my remaining roll of currency and handed it to her, the gesture appallingly insignificant as a means of honoring her part in the passing drama that threatened her life and would surely be seared deep into her psyche long into adulthood. She was the victim of the systematically calculated violence of her environment, a sentence imposed upon her by the circumstances of her birth. For all I knew, her brother was one of the kids brandishing a pistol at me minutes earlier.

She took the bill from me without words, her eyes free of gratitude, and rightfully so. They told me I was one of them, the same as the tribes of youth who wandered her poverty-scorched landscape with pistols in search of some hollow god, whether money or power or adrenaline. I was a combat vet armed with a submachine gun and a shotgun, had a growing list of kills under my belt, and yet I found myself unable to maintain the stare of a little girl.

Tears stung at my eyes, and I blinked them away. Pulling my jacket over the weapons, I passed through the open doorway without looking back at her.

* * *

As I walked uphill through the sweltering tropical heat, I crossed a street that opened into an expansive view that nearly stopped me in my tracks. I looked down a cascading waterfall of shantytown between vivid green mountains, converging in a focal point of clean, orderly skyscrapers silhouetted against the South Atlantic Ocean. It was the same ocean that now separated me from the Dark Continent I'd returned from a mere week ago.

After quickly taking in the sight, I forced myself to continue moving.

To stage another close-range ambush for the chance of slaying our hunters, I'd have to move deeper into the heart of the favela, where the building density was the greatest. I needed only the slightest amount of open space to thin the kill team's ranks. If I could whittle a man or two from their number before the close fight began, my odds of survival went up exponentially.

I hated the favela more with every step I took.

The entire geography was a steep uphill slope, uninhabitable by those who could afford life on flatter ground. My hip flexors were still fatigued after the long march through the African desert, a fact I hadn't paid much mind to until forced to weave my way along buildings clinging for purchase among the hills.

I passed the inverted hulk of a burned-out car, its

charred exterior the only surface in sight devoid of the illegible scrawl of spray paint. The soundtrack in the favela's inner depths was one of feral dogs and screaming children, the smells an ever-shifting tirade of food, garbage, and raw sewage. While the streets and alleyways I'd traversed before were narrow, as I moved deeper they became claustrophobically tight. The ground beneath my feet turned to dirt littered with so many trampled pieces of wood, cardboard, trash, and unidentifiable debris that the collective mass formed a carpet of decay.

And through it all, even as I walked beside a deep gulley hosting a stagnant river of human waste, and faced grave physical danger against men I couldn't be expected to defeat, I somehow found myself thinking of the little girl.

With it came a deep and undeniable regret and shame that I was pursuing a path to revenge that seemed, in the wake of my current circumstances, utterly meaningless.

Perhaps it was just a passing thought that would vanish when and if we emerged alive. There was no other explanation for my feelings of vengeance waning before Karma's body was cold. Before it was cold? She'd been dead five months—five times longer than I'd known her. Yet still I plodded forth on a march to revenge—against what? Boss, Matz, and Ophie would have killed me themselves if I couldn't serve their purposes. In their service I had inadvertently killed Remy, my best friend from the Army. Should I avenge him too by killing myself?

I was no longer a complete stranger to revenge fulfilled. I'd gotten my taste when gunning down Caspian for betraying the team. And that, I reminded myself, had been no Hollywood sunset ending. I'd spent twenty hours in a transcontinental cargo plane beside his body bag, not daring to look inside. What had his death accomplished? It didn't bring back Boss's team or Karma. I wasn't sleeping any better.

My own situation had changed so rapidly—from the Rangers, to West Point, to Boss's team, to fighting for the Outfit first in Somalia and now Brazil, and I'd experienced so much violence along the way, that I'd never stopped to evaluate what truly mattered to me anymore. What would happen if I did?

The truth was, even after waking up in his electric chair, my motivation to kill the Handler was beginning to wane.

If I could live a life free of descent into the omnipresent ether of depression, I would. The team had been gone so long. I'd spent longer trying to avenge them than I'd known them, Karma most of all.

Maybe fatigue was taking over my mind as I passed through a day without sleep and little in the way of food and water to stave off exhaustion. Regardless, Ian's life depended on my actions. If I didn't kill the Handler, Ian would never stop; he'd pursue assassination attempts to the point of self-destruction. He was the last surviving member of the team—it was now about saving him as much as avenging the others. Besides, I reminded myself, I was now in too deep. There was no walking away from my situation, no place on earth I could hide from the Handler.

The little girl's face continued to haunt me. At my core, I knew why: because she made me feel.

I was a killer who had become an actor—flitting among the living, pretending to experience the normal range of human sensation. But emotionally I had gone numb except for rage and despair, the former cultivated in my battles against other men and the latter, myself. A young girl from the favela had sliced through the shroud; whether knowingly or unknowingly to her, I couldn't tell.

And as I knew, anything that allowed me to feel beneath the inner isolation was a prize to behold. Booze, adrenaline, and women had previously occupied the throne in alternating succession. But fundamental human connection and compassion had never played a role until now, and that sudden shift left me walking onward, armed and bewildered, wondering what I had become—and worse yet, what I was becoming still—as my successive fights for survival continued without end.

* * *

The sight of the building in front of me stopped me in my tracks.

Its construction was similar to others in the favela: an unstable red clay brick structure only two stories high, with stems of rebar sprouting from a corrugated iron roof. The sole distinguishing factors were its short height and its solitude, but given what I was about to attempt, the combination of both within the favela made it a boon from the god of war. A few meters of open ground separated it from taller adjacent buildings in all directions, and at first glimpse I knew on some instinctive level that I would either die in its confines or leave it victorious with the key to Parvaneh's rescue.

When I entered the unlocked door, I found out why the building stood alone.

A single man in a sweat-soaked shirt spoke loudly behind a wooden lectern, his eyes pinched shut behind wide-rim glasses, wisps of gray hair combed back from his forehead.

Two dozen congregants were packed into rows of foldout chairs, where they nodded and muttered chants of reverence.

His eyes opened at the conclusion of a sentence, and he looked directly at me before continuing his sermon without a second's hesitation. I pulled my jacket open, exposing the MP5 and breacher shotgun slung against my side. Even then the preacher cautiously finished his sentence, waiting until the next chant of hallelujahs from the audience had fallen silent before addressing me.

"*Você pode se juntar à congregação ou sair.*"

The creaking of metal chairs heralded every occupant in the church turning in their seats to look at me.

I waved a hand over the crowd, and then swung it to the door behind me. "Get out. *Vamos, ahora.* Everyone."

The preacher replied with a heavily accented voice, though his English was crystal. "I said, 'You may join the congregation or leave.' So *you* may choose to stay, or '*vamos.*' But this is a house of God, and no place for weapons."

"I bring weapons everywhere. And you need to get everyone out of here before you find out why that policy makes perfect sense today, Father."

"Pastor," he corrected me. "And we will finish our sermon with or without you."

"If I had any other choice, I wouldn't be here. The sermon's over, Pastor. You don't understand what's coming."

Behind the glasses, his eyes crinkled in a contemptuous grin. "Without judging by appearances, brother, I think the failure to understand is yours. Anyone with business in the hills would not disturb this church."

"If I had a choice, I wouldn't be here."

"Whoever is after you, I can reason with them."

"No, you can't."

"My counsel reaches young men from every gang. Members from the newest recruit to the highest leadership receive my blessing without judgment. Who have you offended—ADA?"

"No, you don't—"

"Red Command? TCP?"

"*Senhor* Ribeiro."

These two words caused him to stop abruptly, squinting as if to make sure he'd heard me correctly. When he spoke again, it was to direct expeditious Portuguese at his congregation.

Their reaction made the import of his words clear enough.

The congregation rose at once, filing out between the rows of foldout chairs and streaming past me on their way out the door—more women than men, more old than young. There was no fear among them and very little surprise. A man with guns had shown up, and they would return once he left. No strangers to violence, their eyes held a disdain for me exceeded only by the girl I'd left behind in her kitchen.

I watched the final elderly congregants shuffle out the door, leaving only the preacher.

"You need to leave too, Pastor. Ribeiro's got a kill team in the favela, and believe me when I tell you that I'm very popular with them right now."

He ignored me, passing down the vacated rows and straightening the foldout chairs as if the service had come to a routine conclusion.

Continuing his task without looking up, he replied, "If

the man you speak of has a kill team looking for you, brother, you should not be standing still, but running."

I thought of the imminent Outfit invasion, the catastrophic effects on an already violence-ravaged population.

I shot back, "If I run, a lot of innocent people here will die before the sun rises. Members of your church among them, Pastor. There are violent men coming for me now, but what follows if I don't face them will be worse."

"Men of violence are one thing I do understand. Before I turned my life over to Jesus, I was one of them. The violence, easy money, the clothes, the guns, the"—he hesitated, his hands frozen on the last chair he'd touched —"the women. I knew it all."

I walked down the center aisle, evaluating the tiny windows, looking for ways in and out. Then I walked behind the pulpit, finding no cover from ballistic trauma and no route to the second floor besides a single stairwell. I stopped at the bottom of the steps, seeing the preacher watching me closely.

Looking upward, I counted twelve steps rising to the second floor. "Scrap everything but the violence and guns, and you just summed up most of my adult life."

"It is not life that should concern you, brother, but the afterlife."

For a moment I was trapped inside the steel drum, sinking into the icy waters of the New Jersey harbor where the Outfit had first tested me. My chest on fire as I held my breath to stave off drowning, hypothermia taking hold as the pressure in my ears became unbearable. Through the holes of my steel tomb, I watched helplessly as the blue glow of the harbor above faded to blackness until, finally, I let the freezing water fill my lungs.

Then my memory turned to the ancient, frail psychologist interviewing me after my resuscitation.

What do you remember from being dead?

I said, "There's no afterlife, Pastor."

"None of us will know until we have crossed over."

"I have crossed over."

He set down the chair and faced me. Then he unfastened the top three buttons of his shirt, pulling the collar to one side to reveal a discolored, oblong bullet scar. "You may have caught a glimpse, yes. But you are still with the living."

"I'm a gunslinger, Pastor." My voice trembled. "If I have a soul, then it's not worth saving anymore."

He buttoned his shirt back up to the collar, smiling to himself. "You want to talk about violence and death? If we were to compare notes, I'd bet I have you beat. But all saints are former sinners. I was once where you are, and if Jesus can do what he's done for me, he can certainly do it for you."

My neck was burning with anticipation. Ribeiro's kill team was drawing closer by the second. I thought of Agustin and said, "The last person to tell me something like that is on his way here now. And you're going to like him a whole lot less than you like me. Now please, go."

He approached me slowly, his stare unwavering, and stopped a few feet away. "Allow me to pray a blessing over you. If there is anyone you need on your side right now, it is a man of God."

"Whatever gets you out of here quicker."

He closed the final gap between us with two quick steps. My grip clamped instinctively on the MP5, but his hands were already clasped on my shoulders, his head bowed inches from my face.

"God, this man is holding onto the power he came from, the power to pull the trigger. Show him that there's a power even greater than that."

I bowed my head with him, looking down to find my hand loosened on the submachine gun as he continued, "I've been there, Lord, I've done that. You've done something radical in my life, and I believe you can do that in this man's life too. May you deliver him from sin and find him worthy to conquer a greater evil."

He looked up, lowering his hands.

"What do you mean," I asked, "find me *worthy*?"

"He has a plan for us all, and that doesn't always match what we intend for ourselves. I'm sorry, brother"— he shrugged and gestured helplessly toward the ceiling —"but in the end, it's up to the Lord."

I stepped back and regained my grip on the MP5, feeling my jaw settle. "There's going to be a lot of shooting. Wait a few hours before you come back. There will be bodies. If mine isn't one of them, you'll know your blessing worked."

He nodded to me. "I hope I see you again and feel the difference God's hand has worked in your life. If not here, then when all the great warriors of eternity are gathered around the fire of heaven. From one gunslinger who renounced the life of bloodshed to another that hopefully shall one day, Godspeed."

I turned from him and trotted up the stairs, inspecting the tight living quarters of the second floor for cover and concealment, and more specifically, to examine the row of stairs leading to a hatch in the roof. Emerging onto the rooftop, I inspected the surrounding buildings before reentering the church, leaving the hatch ajar.

Descending back to the first floor, I found the pastor gone.

I locked the front door from the inside, then trashed his careful arrangement of foldout chairs as quickly as I could, using them to barricade the door in a pile so large that a professional lineman would have to spend considerable time forcing his way through them. Then I moved to a window in the back of the church that was barely wide enough for me to slip past, shimmied through the space with my weapons and backpack, and left.

* * *

They came within the hour.

The first indication of their presence was the same as last night, when my vigil over the signal fires ended in a desperate bid to evacuate Parvaneh, certain that death had arrived to overtake us. And the difference between the arrival of danger and death itself was in the noise—most people responded to danger with the noisy anxiety of panicked masses. But the arrival of death manifested in a different form altogether: silence.

Or as close as one could get in the favela.

The streets suddenly grew as deserted as they had earlier, a shared continuity with Afghanistan and Iraq, when the disappearance of first children and then everyone else preceded gunplay. But the silence within the favela was another phenomenon altogether, when even the irrepressible squalling of infants was more or less muted, with terrified mothers providing comfort in unison.

And only after the deathly silence had descended and

maintained its hold for a full minute did the first man from Ribeiro's kill team come into view.

He moved quickly along the street, his suppressed M4 carried at the low ready. From my hidden vantage point on the second story and twenty-five meters distant, his speed indicated an extreme confidence in his own skills and reaction time. A perfect point man, I thought: first into the line of fire, and by all appearances quite happy to be there.

But the others didn't follow.

I had hoped to pick off a trailing member of the kill team, preferably Agustin—if I could slay only one man in the coming confrontation, I'd make sure it was him. But the point man was alone. He wasn't leading the formation; instead, he was trying to draw fire in a setting where someone could hide a few meters in any direction amid the urban sprawl. That meant the other four shooters were far enough back to maneuver on me the moment I compromised my position.

The point man didn't move straight to the church—he knew that to be a trap. My public seizure of it had been too obvious, so he circled the surrounding area instead, passing in and out of alleys and footpaths off the open space surrounding the building. He was looking for the ambush position he knew waited for him, not appearing too concerned about getting shot in the meantime.

It was an offensive form of reverse ambush, but one that I couldn't pass up. If I didn't take the shot, he was as likely as not to find me first. I had only seconds before he either saw me or disappeared from my view. My plan was about to evaporate, leaving me with a moment-by-moment reaction to an unfolding firefight against overwhelming odds. The only end would be my death or that of the kill team, one of which would occur in the next ninety seconds.

The man's figure passed within the dull black ring of my MP5's front sight, and I centered the vertical spike of the sight post on his femurs before squeezing the trigger. My 9mm rounds and iron sights were woefully insubstantial for precision fire at that distance, so I blasted six rounds from the submachine gun in the hope that at least one would hit its mark.

After the deathly quiet that had befallen the favela, each gunshot sounded like a mini nuclear blast. The point man fell in place. I'd hoped to leave him alive and screaming, letting one or more of his teammates cross into my sights as they tried to save him.

But after falling he fought through the pain, scanning the buildings around him as he spoke into a radio hand mic on his shoulder. Though lying with a probable broken femur and his lifeblood flowing into the vile sludge beneath him, he kept a single-minded focus on spotting my position to vector in his team.

His eyes fell upon my vantage point, where I was curled into a tight sitting position with a knee in my left armpit, support arm braced against my shin. I sat atop a flimsy dining room table situated three feet away from the open window through which I fired three more rounds. The trio of bullets found his head before he could transmit over his radio again.

The kill team's number was reduced to four.

My last shot faded to the snapping of incoming rounds hitting the interior wall beside me. I fell from the table in the kind of unscripted movement that only occurs in gunfights—a burst of animal momentum that propelled me sideways and down with the spontaneity of a startled cat. Crashing onto the kitchen's slick vinyl flooring, I registered that the return fire had come from a direction opposite the point man.

The kill team hadn't moved straight to the church, I realized at once; they had surrounded it from afar and sent one man in to force my hand. Their bid had worked.

I shot upright and bolted through a door leading to the stairwell outside. As I reached it, I could already hear men thundering toward me from below, racing to halt my escape. I leapt up the stairs three at a time, crossing onto the third floor and darting to a short ladder leading to a square opening in the roof.

Scrambling up it, I pulled myself onto the roof's surface, but my blast of relief was halted by the MP5 stock snagging on the opening. The process of moving it and wedging myself through cost me precious seconds marked by the rising fear that I'd get shot in the ass before I succeeded.

And then, with a final clawing pull, I was atop the roof.

I'd barely cleared the opening when the sharp hiss of bullets zipped through it and into the sky. I broke into a run between two cylindrical water tanks. Under perfect circumstances, I could have hidden behind them and fired on my pursuers when they climbed atop the ladder; but the clumsy snag of my submachine gun let them get too close, and now my footsteps were chased by the *plunk* of bullets piercing the corrugated iron below me.

With a frantic quickening of pace, I darted between the water tanks. Reaching the end of the roof, I accelerated my run into a final hard step and jumped.

I only had to clear a few horizontal meters in order to reach an adjacent rooftop set ten feet lower—a feat I could have achieved drunk on any other day. But a sudden, crippling return of pain in my right knee caused it to nearly buckle at the moment of my launch. As a result, my body tumbled through the air, barely clearing a drooping power line strung between buildings.

I managed a pitiful crash landing at the very edge of the church roof, rolling to a near-stop that ended as I began crawling to the hatch that I'd left ajar. If I didn't make it inside before the shooters behind me reached the edge, I'd make a remarkably easy target for them.

But as I pulled myself through the roof hatch and slid down a few interior stairs, I heard no incoming gunfire. Seizing on the opportunity to clamber down the rest of the stairs, I reached the second-floor landing within the church's living area.

This was it, I thought; the culmination of my effort, of pulling danger away from Parvaneh so that I could assume it myself, of preventing the favela invasion and innocent deaths through an act of lunacy, or suicide, or both. This was what I did, the one thing I excelled at if nothing else. I readied the MP5 across my chest and took a few panting breaths as I waited for their next move. They could either leap onto the church roof and assault downward or hit the ground floor and fight their way up.

To my horror, they did both.

An explosion on the ground floor rattled the building, its blast so loud within the confined space that I couldn't tell whether it was a grenade or a breaching charge on the front door. I didn't have time to consider it further as a man smashed against the roof.

I pivoted up the stairs and toward the roof hatch with the MP5, hoping to shoot the jumper before he had time to recover from the impact. But his partner on the opposite roof was covering the hatch, and the zipping impact of incoming bullets slicing through the roof and into the stairwell forced me down onto the second floor, where I could hear men crashing through the front door and past my barricade of chairs.

Looking up to the ceiling, I knew that the first man would now cover the hatch as the second jumped onto the roof. I was trapped between two-man assault teams, one above and one below.

I put the MP5 on fully automatic, elevating its barrel to the ceiling.

I had about twenty rounds remaining in the magazine, and as the clatter of a second man hitting the roof echoed above me, I aimed at the noise and unleashed all of them.

A man cried out and then went silent by the end of my burst. Before I could reload, the hatch was darkened by the shadow of the first man, who began firing down the stairs and into the second floor.

I threw my back against the wall under the stairs as bullets darted through the space. Grabbing the slung shotgun, I turned and cast its barrel upward at the hatch. The roar of the first 12-gauge blast erupted, and the flame from the shot receded to a view of a mangled human ankle on the top stair. Pumping the shotgun, I whirled toward a shadow racing up the stairway and fired into the wall to halt his progress. Another pump of the shotgun as I spun to face the man from the roof, now sliding down the stairs on one functional leg with a strange expression of composure as he fought for control of his M4.

Bringing the shotgun to his face, I fired at near point-blank range.

Without waiting to see the effect, I faced the stairs and charged the shotgun again, this time firing my final shell to momentarily prevent the last two men from assaulting upward.

A man shot his M4 wildly around the corner of the stairs—if the kill team had previously cared about taking me alive, I'd since goaded them out of it. The neatly painted walls around me were suddenly marred with the thwacking slice of incoming bullets. The pair of men assaulting from the ground knew their teammates were out of the fight and decided to fire everything they had around the corner.

I couldn't make it to the roof without getting shot, so instead I grabbed the dead man from the stairs and pulled him to the floor. Leaping on his back and grabbing his shoulders, I rolled him atop me and hoisted us into a semi-seated position against the wall.

Rounds were ricocheting everywhere now, both my shotgun and MP5 empty. I reached for the M4 slung across the dead body in front of me, but its sling was pinned between us and I couldn't force the barrel upward.

I dropped the rifle and fumbled across his chest from behind, feeling across pouches until I found the spherical mass I was looking for.

Tearing the pouch open, I withdrew a fragmentation grenade, pulled the pin, and let the spoon fly off. After letting another second of suppressed gunfire elapse, I hurled the grenade down the stairs.

The gunfire ended with a man's shrill scream cut short by the grenade blast. The reverberating howl of the explosion receded to the sound of running footsteps below.

A final man had survived the detonation, racing down the stairs and out the front door. My sudden turn of fate had brought with it the onslaught of euphoria that followed unlikely victory over death. This time, however,

that rush came with an overwhelming sense of omnipotence, of immortality taking hold in a split-second fractal
of time.

Effortlessly flinging the dead man's bulk off my body, I
grabbed his M4 sling and tore it over the bloody mass of
his mangled head. My right knee burned as I moved up
the steps with a speed that I shouldn't have been capable
of. My two slung weapons clattered at my side as I
emerged on the roof, covered in the slick of another man's
blood, giving no consideration to his partner that I'd shot
through the ceiling and whether he may be alive and
aiming at me. A preternatural sense of confidence assured
me he was dead—they all were, save one that I was about
to kill in my final act of dominion over this impossible
combat engagement.

Nothing could stop me now. I'd singlehandedly pulled
a looming danger away from Parvaneh, had faced death at
every turn, and yet saved both her and the little girl I'd
encountered in the interim. I'd gone to the dark center of
the favela to clash with a monster of overwhelming
proportions and won. I'd been drowned and returned to
life, had reached my current position in the Outfit for a
reason. This reminder brought with it the words of the
psychologist who spoke to me after my resurrection: *I
think you'll go far in this business, if they let you in.*

And upon my return to North America, I would kill
the Handler.

I neared the edge of the roof in seconds, sighting the
fleeing figure of the last man and taking aim at once. He
had almost vanished into a darkened alleyway by the time
the rifle optic had met my line of sight, and for the briefest
of moments I thought I saw him pairing with a sixth man
in the shadows. Both figures instantly disappeared in the

muzzle blast of my M4 as I emptied the remaining rounds in the magazine with rapid single shots.

When the weapon ran out of ammo, I focused through the optic to see the prize due to me, the visual gratification of bodies and blood that I knew waited beyond.

There was nothing.

They were gone.

"*FUCK YOU!*" I yelled, savagely throwing the empty M4 down beside me.

The fifth man had escaped, possibly with a sixth, and I felt a desperate pang of urgency to learn whether one of them was Agustin. I spun and moved to the other man on the roof, his body lying face down.

I'd fired close to twenty rounds through the corrugated iron ceiling in the hope that one would find a kill shot. I'd succeeded with two—one that exited the base of his brain, and another that crested the top of his head, scalping him and allowing an ooze of fluid to pour onto the metal roof and drain into the nearest trio of bullet holes.

I rolled his body over, hoping to see Agustin's face, but found a clean-shaven jaw with a sideways entry wound instead.

Releasing the body in disgust, I stood and made for the stairs, descending them unarmed and past the dead man I had used for cover from the incoming bullets. I had seen his face in the second before I blasted it with the shotgun and knew he wasn't the man I met outside Ribeiro's office.

I'd watched the point man closely before shooting him, so that left a single grenade victim on the stairs for me to check. All my rage in that moment was directed against Agustin, and I felt an irrational desire to confirm his death. It wasn't that he tried to kill me—that much was fair play. But the intimate conversation he'd held with me, getting to know his quarry before the police ambush and ultimate pursuit through the favela, left me wanting him dead as much as anyone I'd felt wrath for in the past.

I stormed down the stairs completely unarmed, two useless weapons at my side, driven to the point of sense-lessness. A billowing fog of smoke and incinerated clay brick flowed, stinking and choking, up the stairs and toward the roof hatch. Taking a breath and holding it as I plunged into the cloud, I found the last body just around the corner of the stairs, his firing position becoming the last place he'd occupied in life.

The back of his head was remarkably unscathed, torso intact between twin plates of body armor. But the grenade had bounced off the brick walls and detonated behind him, leaving his body from the waist down an indistin-guishable mass of scorched flesh.

Grabbing his hair and pulling his head up, I saw a life-less stranger staring back at me through the haze.

I released him, my head suddenly pounding with exertion. Taking a desperate breath, I coughed stinking lungfuls of air thick with explosive residue and brick dust and smoking human flesh.

Climbing the stairs back to the landing, I was over-come with a sudden insatiable thirst for water. I fell to my hands and knees beneath the fog of destruction that billowed overhead.

In that moment, the entire mass of my troubled exis-tence descended on me at once: Boss's team and Karma and Caspian, Remy's face before I killed him, the pain I'd endured before and after wars both military and criminal, the deception of life lived as a lie. My suicide forestalled, for anyone else a symbol of hope but for me a meaning-less achievement that resulted in the deaths of so many others.

And for what?

A mental image of the psychologist's bulging, ice-blue eyes upon me after my drowning. *You're here for a reason, son. And you need to remind yourself of that reason every day of your life.*

And then the pastor.

May you deliver him from sin, and find him worthy to conquer a greater evil.

I threw up a bitter stream of bile and then slid to a semi-collapsed position beside it, keeping below the smoke to take sobbing breaths of air. Rolling over to my side, I felt my hand hit the man I'd blasted in the face with the shotgun. He was on his stomach now, the back of his body armor revealing the rows of pouches I'd glimpsed while hiding in the cabinet of the favela kitchen.

One of them formed a perfect rectangular shape, sharp edges ending in the stubby protrusion of a short-whip radio antenna.

6

_____

From behind the mountains a ruby glow descended, pulling a veil of darkness in its wake.

I should have been running. The sunset was imminent now, and with it an Outfit invasion. Every encroaching inch of darkness decreased my likelihood of linking up with Micah and the helicopter's ability to spot us amid the rooftops of a million sprawling shanties. But between the weight of my backpack bouncing like a pendulum and the burning pain in my right knee, my gait had settled into a shuffling jog.

The people of the favela parted before me. I couldn't imagine how insane I looked to them—a blood-soaked gringo going on thirty-six hours awake, plummeting down the hill in the excruciating clutch of an adrenaline hang-over. If someone started shooting at me, all pain would be lifted, and I'd once again gain the superhuman abilities of speed and coherence under duress. Until then, I grunted through the full gamut of joints and muscles strained too hard for too long in the fight for survival.

I'd performed a hasty search of the kill team, who had

far more equipment than I could carry in my small back-pack. I took the essential items in pairs, my bag becoming an ark for twin radios and GPS, along with spare maga-zines. Then I took two M4s, slinging one over my shoulder for Micah and carrying the other in my hands. I was beyond the need or even ability to conceal weapons, and the shotgun and MP5 had been left behind in lieu of supe-rior firepower.

The outskirts of the favela that had initially struck me as the pit of destitution now appeared comparatively luxurious after escaping the dense area surrounding the church. I passed a few barren trees rising from patches of dirt between slabs of asphalt, the sight a paragon of natural wonder. Even the phone and power lines converging like spider webs across mildew-caked build-ings that had seemed so imposing upon our arrival now appeared comforting symbols of familiarity.

As the sunlight waned, I cursed Micah for not telling me the emergency frequency that the Outfit would moni-tor. But fearing my capture, he had adamantly protected it. Even his link-up plan was fraught with precaution for Parvaneh. I was to carry my weapon left-handed if being followed or proceeding under duress, right-handed if not, as I traveled down the favela's equivalent of a parking lot, where the partially paved road bore cars and motorcycles crammed into every possible space.

A sharp whistle to my right stopped me dead in my tracks. Whirling toward the noise, I ducked between people and approached a makeshift storefront with a closed roll-up door. Then I heard the whistle again, softer this time. I followed the noise to a footpath between struc-tures, where Micah stepped out from the shadows.

The short protrusion of an MP5 barrel halted my

progress as he leveled it at my chest. His eyes were ablaze, certain that the kill team would plunge into the space after me. Sending me out and moving his primary involved a catastrophic degree of risk, second only to bringing me back in proximity to her.

"What happened?" he asked.

I held my palms up to him. "I've got radios. There's still one man from the kill team out there, maybe two."

He lowered the gun, cautiously eyeing the road behind me. "Come on."

I followed him as he trotted down the footpath, cutting left through a row of steel drums and crouching to slide behind a stack of sheet metal leaned against the wall. The stack concealed a manhole-sized tunnel that I felt my way through, my backpack scraping against the low ceiling.

We crossed onto the other side of the wall into a cavernous space bathed in shadows. Micah erected a wobbly ladder from the ground, planting it against a second-story platform. Then he shot up it as I struggled to keep pace with my injured knee, relying on my opposite leg and upper body to haul myself upward.

We entered a partially finished third floor atop the current structure. Concrete pillars separated floor beams from the uninstalled sheets of corrugated iron balanced above. Micah knocked the ladder sideways, letting it crash to the ground. Then he moved to the corner of a wall and whispered, "Nightingale."

"Raven," Parvaneh's voice said from beyond.

We rounded the wall to see Parvaneh crouched in the corner, lowering the Beretta. My eyes stalled on her a moment too long.

How did I ever think this woman wasn't beautiful? She

was stunning, the radiance of her eyes arresting my attention. My focus shifted to her angelic, peaceful face and her long, lean body rising to stand before me.

Forcing myself to break my gaze, I unslung the M4s and the backpack and then unzipped it, pawing for the radios and setting them down beside the bag.

Micah grabbed one of them, thumbing the keys to change frequency as I placed a GPS beside him.

I set an M4 on the ground and split the magazines between us as Micah began speaking into the hand mic. "Silver Bullet, Silver Bullet, this is Jaguar Actual."

No response.

"Silver Bullet, Jaguar Actual."

The hand mic crackled, and a tinny voice responded, *"Jaguar Actual, this is Silver Bullet. Send your traffic."*

He lifted the GPS off the ground, reading the latitude and longitude in careful phonetic pronunciation. Once he relayed our location, he finished with, "Primary and two pax ready for pickup time now, rooftop LZ marked by Jaguar Actual, how copy?"

"Bullet copies all, helo is en route. ETA six minutes."

Parvaneh and I locked eyes. Her expression still held an air of thankfulness, now mixed with immense relief. I couldn't match it. For some reason I suddenly thought back to Karma in the seat beside me, making our final hopeful eye contact in the moment before she was killed.

The thought disappeared as Micah addressed me. "We've got a landing area on the roof next door. I'm going there to flag down the bird. Go back the way we came and make sure no one puts the ladder up and tries to follow us. Pull security toward the alley until you hear the helo coming in. When you do, escort Parvaneh to me."

"Micah, man, I thought you were the bodyguard."

"Save it."

"I mean, how about that landing area? I called it, we moved, and if we stayed in that hole in the ground we'd probably be dead right now."

"David—"

"Seriously, do I get paid extra for this?"

"Go. Now."

He waited for me to move, handing Parvaneh the MP5 and taking the spare M4 for himself. I put on the backpack and turned to leave, stopping at the corner to see him vanish out of sight around an unfinished wall.

Parvaneh watched me, looking mildly amused. "Well?"

I shot her a wink before rounding the wall, moving back the way I'd come.

Turning the corner, I did a double take.

The top of the ladder now rose over the edge of the floor as if Micah hadn't knocked it down.

Then the ladder moved—slightly at first, then a sudden shift nearly an inch sideways. Someone was ascending toward me, and with Micah securing the landing zone and Parvaneh between us, I was the only thing standing between her and an unseen aggressor. Karma sprang to mind again, and my body burned with boiling, visceral hatred. I wasn't going to fail a woman under my protection a second time.

My M4 raised itself toward the ladder as I stalked toward it, all pain forgotten, creeping silently until I took a knee a few feet away.

The ladder moved again.

In a rush of exhilaration, I realized that the man on the ladder had to be Agustin. His retreat from the devastated church was no cowardly bid to escape with his life—

I should have known as much from his calmness during Ribeiro's meeting. Instead, his withdrawal was a tactical ploy, and a brilliant one at that. He'd not risked getting shot while facing his opponent with equal odds. Down to himself, he'd simply followed me back to her, and was now coming to claim the ultimate prize.

My thumb rested atop the selector lever of my M4. I didn't dare flick it off safe and risk betraying my vigil until the instant before I fired. I waited for his bearded face to appear, relishing the opportunity to observe him in the pregnant pause before I drilled a 5.56 round through his forehead.

A hand appeared on the top rung—even if the other held a pistol, he'd never beat my reaction time to the first shot. The top of his head cleared the edge, and I waited for the face to appear before clicking my assault rifle to fire, my index finger pulling the slack out of the trigger before I stopped abruptly.

It was Gabriel.

His perpetually nervous face turned a ghastly shade of white as he reluctantly drank in the sight of a suppressor inches from his face. Lips trembling, he kept a hand on the top rung and raised the other to reveal an open palm, fingers quivering.

I lowered the barrel before he fell off the ladder. "Where the fuck have you been?"

"I...I dove into a pile of trash and hid...I've been looking for you all day, until I saw you running down the street. I almost missed you and Micah turning into the alley."

"Anyone follow you?"

"No, I...I don't think so..."

I stood and stepped to the edge, sweeping the low

ground with my M4's optic. The space between structures was dark in the fading light, but I would have been able to distinguish a human form.

"Hurry up," I said, "the helo will be here any minute."

I used a free hand to grab his wrist and hoist him over the edge, and then kicked the ladder sideways until it fell askew once more.

Holding the shoulder of his shirt, I pulled him toward the corner of the wall and said, "Nightingale."

"Raven," Parvaneh replied.

We turned the corner to see her standing out in the open, lowering the MP5 as she looked from me to Gabriel.

I spun and left them together, stalking around the wall. Returning to my position beside the ladder's previous resting place, I took a knee with the M4. The odds of anyone returning to right the ladder were slim to none, but I couldn't take any chances. If anyone was going to make a last-minute bid to take her life, it was Agustin. I thought of his sprint from the building toward the alley, where I'd seen him possibly link up with a sixth man just before I opened fire.

The sixth man.

My blood ran cold.

I was back to the corner in seconds, this time forgoing the verbal challenge and password as I noiselessly angled around the edge.

Parvaneh faced away from me, her near-black hair cascading to her shoulders toward the Beretta stuffed into her waistband. The MP5 was slung at her side and her hands were open, palms skyward as if gesturing.

Tilting my head sideways another fraction of an inch, I saw Gabriel a few feet away, his quaking hands pointing a revolver at her chest.

I took a single step and launched myself airborne, hurling into Parvaneh with all the strength I could muster as I twisted my rifle sideways toward him.

Gabriel reacted to my appearance with alarming speed, turning the revolver to me as I flicked my weapon to full auto. I only caught a single word Gabriel murmured before we opened fire on each other. It hung in the space between us in the fragment of time before my shoulder impacted Parvaneh to knock her out of the way.

"...sorry."

I mashed my trigger as his revolver erupted in volcano blasts of fire.

Adrenaline should have delayed the onset of pain, but it didn't.

The bullets were white-hot nails inside me, radiating a vibrating, electric agony throughout my flesh. My body betrayed me as I fell, my determination lost along with control of my motor functions.

I tried to rise and failed. Clutching at the hot wetness seeping across my torso, I raised a bare hand to my face with impossible slowness. My fingers appeared grotesque, foreign, coated in slick crimson blood as if it were a glove. Was the bleeding arterial? I couldn't tell.

I made no valiant effort to defend myself from being shot again, or to face my assailant. In the seconds that I fought to stay awake, my view was encompassed by my own blood spreading across the floor. I laid my head against the ground, the simple act of closing my eyes an indescribable bliss that stopped the physical agony altogether.

An ethereal white mist replaced my vision. It seeped in from the periphery until I could no longer see the ocean of stark red in which I floated, adrift.

MIDNIGHT

Fluctuat nec mergitur

-It is tossed by the waves but it does not sink

7

Boss, Matz, Ophie, and Caspian stood side-by-side, arms around one another. A fifth figure joined them from the periphery: it was Karma, in a cutoff denim skirt and halter top exposing the extent of her tattoos. A sixth figure sauntered in from the left, putting his arm around Karma with a kiss on her cheek and a lopsided grin.

It was me.

Was this death? It couldn't be. It was too clean, too slick, defying the depth of machinations of my troubled psyche, tranquil compared to what my mind was capable of at its darkest pits.

At the same time, I had no connection to a physical form. My consciousness was weightless, grounded neither by gravity nor worldly perception. I was an aura, a shadow upon earth, if I existed there at all.

They were standing before me, but their voices echoed down a hallway of sound.

Their figures faded, then reappeared at the end of a tunnel. The edges were blurred, distorted, as I struggled to focus. I heard them, but it took a moment to register.

Karma broke ranks with the row of men.

You're the only person I've ever met who doesn't believe in God but still hates him.

What?

After this is over, come back to Savannah with me.

Ophie cut her off. *If murder ain't fun, we're doing it wrong.*

Couldn't be an out-of-body experience because my world was spinning again. Too much bourbon? Falling down the stairs on a Wednesday night—time to cut back. Have to piss, bladder about to explode. Nothing but bourbon on the rocks since noon.

Luka's voice screaming, *IT WASN'T ME! IT WAS THE IRANIAN!*

Ophie with his knife to Luka's throat. *Say hello to Caspian for us.*

I asked, who's the Iranian?

Matz answered. *He's dead already. Stop talking.*

The view blasted back to a foggy morning on the farm of my boyhood: the Virginia air cool and damp, a morning mist just beginning to lift as I followed my father through the wet grass of our backyard.

My father stopped at the fence, picking up three tin cans riddled with pencil-width holes and setting them back atop the fencepost. Stepping back, he wiped his fingertips dry on his flannel shirt.

"A rifle can hide your inadequacies, compensate for them with a long barrel, with precise sights, with managed recoil. A rifle is your wife—steady, reliable, the one who cooks and raises your children. A pistol," he continued, reaching into his pocket to pull out a tiny handgun before locking the slide to the rear, "is a mistress. Happy birthday, David."

I took the pistol from his outstretched hand.

Boss spoke next. *And that was the Handler himself, not his assistant.*

What's the mission?

To kill them all.

Ian's voice. *The world isn't big enough to hide his enemies. A challenge to his organization is an open-ended death contract that can't be bought or backed out of.*

"What's a mistress?" my youthful voice asked.

My father answered, "It means the ability to use one is highly perishable, they're hard to control, and if you don't watch your step and master her she can bring your whole world down around you. You can lie to a rifle, but never a pistol—it will highlight your every shortcoming, not conceal them."

Matz now. *There were six of us when we started, and Ophie wasn't one of them. Boss and I were there from the beginning, and so were four others who died along the way. Caspian was just the last to get killed.*

Caspian stepped before me. *Sergio chose a good crop to interview for this job.*

Did Sergio recruit you, too?

No, I had this Iranian dude named Roshan—

"Dad, this is a toy."

"The fundamentals don't change, boy. If you master this little .32 pistol, then one day you can shoot anything. Even my .44 Magnum."

"Is there anything bigger than that?"

"Sure. There's a .454 Casull that'll make my .44 feel like a BB gun."

"Then that's what I want."

My father replied, "Son, a .454 revolver would take

your arm off. Master the .32, and we'll move you up from there."

"But a .454 is the best."

"No, it's just the *biggest*. Have you learned about Franz Ferdinand in school?"

"No. Who's he?"

"His assassination started the First World War. Tens of millions of people died because of a single round fired by a pistol no bigger than the one you hold in your hand. Don't underestimate the little guns, son."

Boss next. *You think the Handler doesn't bleed? We could get to him, too, if we took the time. But if any of us survived the effort, it wouldn't be for long.*

I'm going to kill him.

Why?

Who cares.

I told you to be careful, David. Because this is the view. Have you had the ship dream yet?

Twice.

Has it sunk beneath the wave?

Yes. In Somalia.

Then you're next.

Rolling mist swept before me as if smoke from a fire, erasing them from view with a ghostly hiss of air. A sensation of lightness overtook my body, now floating to the surface in a blurry pool of subconscious thought.

8

I awoke suddenly, my return to awareness bringing with it a clawing search for my M4. But an explosion of pain paralyzed me, and as I fought through it with a rocketing heart rate, I looked up, expecting to see Gabriel stepping over my body to aim his revolver at my face.

But the ceiling was no longer the primitive corrugated iron of a favela roof. Instead it was a technological marvel, a cylindrical metal hull bearing infinite wires and tubes snaking across its surface.

I was off the ground though still horizontal, lying behind a blue curtain beside a row of shelves bearing neatly ordered packs of medical supplies.

My legs were flat atop a stretcher, my upper body propped into a reclined position. Looking down, I saw my left bicep held rigid by a moldable field splint and wrapped within a sling, its strap tightened to pin my left forearm against my stomach. My left shoulder above the splint was buried beneath medical dressings, while my right bore only white gauze and a small amount of medical tape. Black straps were buckled with seatbelt fasteners across my ankles and waist, the latter assembly joined by two shoulder straps.

A clear IV tube ran into my forearm, and I could feel the catheter shift in my vein as I bent and straightened my right arm. I flexed my hand, feeling only the slightest buzz of objection from whatever wound lurked beneath the bandage on my shoulder. When I pulled my hand back I saw that it was clean except for the blood caked deep beneath my fingernails.

I realized I was on a cargo plane in flight, the vibrating hum making it impossible to distinguish any voices beyond the curtain of my medical area. My mind pulsed backwards through the nightmarish sequence of dreams I'd just awoken from, trying to determine what had happened before I'd lost consciousness. I clearly remembered glimpsing Gabriel pointing a gun at Parvaneh, followed by my leap through time and space as I tried to shoulder-check her out of the way while shooting him. He opened fire first, and while I recalled pulling my trigger with the weapon on full auto, the tremendous pain of getting shot erased all else from memory.

Had I knocked Parvaneh out of the line of fire? Had I saved her, or had Gabriel finished her off and left me for dead? Micah hadn't gone far to await the helicopter, and the sound of gunfire would have brought him racing back to Parvaneh's side. Gabriel had either escaped or been killed, but there was no alternate universe in which he could possibly outshoot Micah.

The Handler was going to kill me upon my return no matter what, I remembered; if Parvaneh was dead, the amount of torture preceding that would increase exponentially. He'd assured me of that much in no uncertain terms before my departure. Hell, if Parvaneh was dead, I might save him the trouble. Karma's death was too much to bear, and I couldn't survive if Parvaneh's name was added to the tally of my failure.

Then I thought of my father, and the world war that began from a single pistol shot.

Where was the .32 handgun?

Whatever my circumstances, I wouldn't be left alone for long. Mustering my focus from the fog of sleep, I looked for my backpack with increasing panic.

The field splint around my left bicep was a type I knew well from my Army medical training. In combat we'd always kept the casualty's equipment with their body, whether wounded or dead. Nothing was abandoned to the battlefield, and serial-numbered military hardware was never left to chance. In my case, the backpack held sensitive radios and GPS from Ribeiro's kill team that some technical division would certainly be waiting to exploit upon landing.

But I saw only prearranged medical supplies lining the wall along with a few canvas fold-down seats. If the backpack had been kept with me, it had to be under my stretcher.

With one functional arm, I impulsively unbuckled the fasteners pinning me to the stretcher at the waist. Then I leaned forward, reaching for the final strap at my ankles.

The pain that had immobilized me on wakeup suddenly struck once more. My left bicep felt like sledge-hammers were pummeling it, razor-sharp splinters of bone slicing through liquefied flesh. The rush of pain caused a great wave of dizziness that nearly made me fall back in defeat.

I took a breath and fought through the torment, realizing that the slightest shift in the sling pinning my left arm resulted in pure agony. The clear IV tube stretched taut against my right arm, nearly pulling the catheter out as my fingertips crested the buckle at my ankles and unfastened it.

I threw the straps aside, trying to keep my left arm stationary as I rotated my body sideways out of the stretcher. I set my feet on the vibrating floor of the aircraft, my mind spinning with a wave of lightheadedness, and knelt to look below the stretcher, my right knee aflame as I searched for my bag.

The sight of an empty platform between the stretcher's four locked wheels caused me to nearly scream and flip the stretcher. As the rage of helplessness peaked, I saw that a fifth, stabilizing wheel assembly emerged from the stretcher's angled headrest.

On an elevated platform attached to it, I saw the backpack.

I barely recognized it at first. The exterior was so stained with dried blood that it was now almost entirely a crusted shade of brown, its straps hacked apart by medical shears. Pinning it against my sling despite the stabbing waves of pain, I used my right hand to pull the zipper open but found the backpack a deflated mass of canvas robbed of its contents. I felt for the interior pouch, desperately hoping the .32 had survived a cursory search.

With a rush of elation, my fingers found it.

I pulled the tiny pistol from the bag. The magazine was still inserted. Not daring to be caught with it, I slipped it into the sling around my left arm, the metallic shape fitting neatly between my wrist and abdomen.

Zipping the bag mostly shut, I shoved it back into its resting place. I pulled myself up by a metal rail, grunting against a throbbing right knee and left arm that battled for my attention. Standing fully, I rotated with my back to the stretcher to keep the clear IV tubing untangled. I only had to get back in the stretcher and buckle myself in before I was in the clear.

"What the fuck are you doing?"

I whirled toward a large man entering through the opening in the curtain, expecting to encounter Micah's enraged stare.

Instead, I saw it was Reilly.

He was in tactical fatigues without any other equipment, his face holding far more authority than when he'd picked me up at the Rio airport.

"I, uh..." I stammered.

"I step out for two minutes to use the john and you're waltzing around my treatment site. Get your dumb ass back on the stretcher."

He helped me back on, and I tried to appear casual as I laid my upper body on the elevated headrest. The pain was excruciating.

"What happened to Parvaneh?" I asked.

He finished situating me, leaving the buckles undone as he nodded to one of the empty canvas fold-down seats. "She was sitting right here until she got called to the cockpit. Thought I'd never get to piss. Matter of fact, I need to let her know you're awake."

"So she's okay?"

"Minor lacerations and a few contusions. Same with Micah."

"Did Gabriel get away?"

"Get away?" He chuckled softly, dropping into a fold-down seat as his face assumed the same boyish enthusiasm as when I'd first met him. "His body's in a bag by the tail, bro. You drilled him in the chest with four rounds before he took you out."

I breathed a sigh of relief. "I was afraid he survived."

"Traitor's justice. What's your pain level at, brother? Need something else to take the edge off?"

"I don't feel anything," I lied.

"You're looking pretty goddamn pale, man."

"Yeah? Well maybe that's because I had the worst dreams of my fucking life from whatever you gave me."

He grinned. "Don't blame me, bro. You got plenty of Midazolam to keep you from having a bad trip, but it took a lot to snow you out."

"English, motherfucker. I feel like I'm back in the favela."

"You're coming out of the K-hole."

"Ketamine?"

"Plus a few re-doses—you kept writhing around, man. You must work out your liver a lot."

I nodded distantly, wincing as I adjusted my arm in the sling. "Did the rest of the delegation get hit?"

"Nope. Evacuated from the country as soon as the four musketeers went missing."

"How bad are my injuries?"

"You made out better than Gabriel. One bullet grazed your right shoulder, one lodged in the meat of your left deltoid. But the moneymaker hit your left bicep and fractured your humerus. You're looking at retained hardware, plate, and screws to hold the bone in place. I'd say three months in a cast, six before you're functional—"

"I should have seen it coming."

"Knock it off. No one saw it coming. He'd been working for the Organization long enough. Micah would have let him in, too." He paused, considering whether to finish his thought, and decided to go ahead anyway. "Searched him for a weapon after he mysteriously returned, probably, but still let him in."

"Were you guys going to invade?"

"Fuckin' A. Whole Outfit's been mobilizing in Rio since you guys went off the grid yesterday. First wave of shooters was an hour from takeoff when Micah's call came."

"Sorry to ruin it for you."

"Ruin it? I'm riding this plane back to Brazil after I drop you guys off. The rest of the Outfit never left. The Handler has already approved the first set of target packets against Ribeiro's organization, so missions start in forty-eight hours. We're going to war."

"Drop us off...where?"

"The Mist Palace. We're an hour from landing. Handler ordered the plane to his personal airstrip."

I gasped for breath, eyes returning to the ceiling.

My pulse was soaring. The field splint around my left arm was constructed from sheets of foam around a thin layer of aluminum. I'd be unable to pass the sweep of a hand-held metal detector, with or without the pistol—and since Parvaneh was alive, that single fact was the ticket to my successful assassination of my greatest enemy.

The thin metal frame of the .32 pistol suddenly felt like a living scorpion wedged between my left wrist and the sling, something small and deadly that would kill at the slightest provocation. In my current circumstances, the thrill of its presence was oddly reassuring.

"Sure you don't want a bit more juice, man? Your arm probably feels okay because it's immobilized and pulling traction. Once you start moving around, you might change your mind real fast."

"I'm fine for now, thanks." Terrified that he'd perceive something out of the ordinary, I said, "I just need to rest some more, man. Seriously."

The curtain was whisked open.

This time it *was* Micah, looking significantly cleaned up from the favela excursion, though his expression of general disdain, particularly when it fell upon me, remained largely intact. He saw first that I was awake, and then checked the unfastened buckles of my stretcher.

"Nice to see you too," I offered.

He said nothing, stepping aside to let Parvaneh in.

Her tall, graceful body stepped into view. She wore clean clothes over her athletic frame, and for all her vulnerability while we were on the run, she had now returned to her full regal air. Hair pulled into a tight ponytail, face spotless and devoid of eye makeup, she swung a piercing gaze to Reilly.

He blurted, "I was about to get you, ma'am. David just woke up."

"Leave us."

"Yes, ma'am." Reilly stepped around them and out of the medical area, and Micah tugged the curtain shut. He stood over me as Parvaneh took a seat, directing her electric green eyes to mine.

I began, "I'm sorry for letting him in—"

"Stop, David. If you didn't, I would have." She looked at my arm in the sling. "I owe you a debt of gratitude for your heroism."

"No, you don't. I'd been looking for an excuse to shoot that little bastard the whole trip."

"How are you feeling?"

"Never better. But there's something I didn't get a chance to tell you two—the guy who took us up the elevator to the meeting with Ribeiro was on the kill team. Agustin. He was the one that got away."

Micah spoke for the first time. "You're certain?"

"One hundred percent. What do you make of that?"

Parvaneh said, "What do we make of any of this? Why did Ribeiro bother meeting with us if he was going to send us to our deaths anyway? Why expose himself just to hear the Handler's terms?"

I said, "Maybe someone else needed to hear them."

"What do you mean?" she asked.

"Ribeiro's not dumb. If he's not capable of taking on the Handler by himself, then he must have a hidden ally who is. Maybe the attempt to kill you was contingent on a mutual agreement with another organization."

Parvaneh shook her head. "None of our allies would betray us. And none are powerful enough to attempt it."

"That doesn't mean some other organization hasn't been rising from the shadows."

"We'd know about that."

"Would you? Look at Gabriel." I paused as a sudden wave of lightheadedness rushed over me. "Let's not forget his picture wasn't on the bounty even though he was in the negotiation with you two. Maybe this is all the brink of something bigger."

Micah gave me a suspicious grin. "Getting shot has turned you into quite the strategist."

"Jealous that I got the save? Certainly sounds like it."

"*Got the save*? Are you out of your mind? You nearly got her shot."

"Micah, leave him alone—"

"Yeah, Micah," I said, "leave me alone." The plane shuddered mid-flight, a brief wave of turbulence punctuating my words.

"You honestly believed that Gabriel just happened upon us?" Micah demanded. "You didn't even *think* to check him for a weapon?"

"Easy for you to say after he shot me."

"It's not you I'm worried about. But your valor is meaningless when you nearly got an ambassador killed in the first place—"

"*ENOUGH!*" Parvaneh said. "I believed Gabriel as readily as David. His failure to check a member of our delegation was equally mine."

When her eyes left mine for Micah's, I flashed a victorious smile.

His face reflected the slight, and Parvaneh didn't care for this shift in his expression.

"Micah, leave us."

He looked torn, though in that moment I wasn't sure who was more uncomfortable, him or me. Casting a sidelong glance toward me that didn't meet my eyes, instead lingering on my chest, he turned and left.

She looked back to me. Her green pupils glowed between dark eyelashes, the effect mesmerizing, hypnotic. Was I attracted to her, or was she merely the living embodiment of Karma, of Laila, my ex-fiancée, of all the women who had been lost to me?

"David, we're going to war. And I want you to be a part of it."

I nodded toward my arm in the sling. "It might be a while before I can shoot."

"I'm counting on it. I want you to join my office in the Organization. You can learn diplomacy and still be involved in planning missions during your recovery."

"You've got better people than me, I'm sure."

She set the fingertips of one hand atop the medical dressing on my shoulder. "No. I don't."

"Parvaneh, I hate to be the one to tell you this, but... your employer is going to finish the job he started before sending me to Rio. I can promise you that much."

"Don't be so sure. I have more influence with the Handler than you know."

"Not *that* much influence."

"Have you considered that he's grooming me?"

"As his ambassador?"

"As his successor."

Every wound in my body simmered at once.

"You're not."

"I am."

"You can't be..."

"His daughter?" She smiled, and I fell silent. The implication of her words echoed in my skull as she continued, "I am. And if I want you spared, I can make that deal. If I tell him that I want you working under me, it will be done."

I found myself shaking my head before I realized what I was doing. "Why serve him? You hate him, that much was clear in the favela."

"His methods are ruthless, but he's an improvement over many who came before him."

"What about your kid? Why are you traipsing around the world getting shot at with a daughter waiting for you?"

"I'm doing what's best for Langley."

"Getting out would be best for her. And you." My mind filled with a vision of the little girl in the favela kitchen. I watched her as my next words found their way out in a near whisper. "What if there was a way, Parvaneh?"

"Out of the Organization?"

"Yes. What if you could take Langley and...leave?"

"David, I could take my daughter and walk away any day I choose. And that's his worst nightmare."

"Why?"

"He believes that I'm the rightful heiress and the Organization will fail without a true bloodline. My daughter and I are the only two people he would never hurt, no matter the circumstances."

I couldn't believe what I was hearing. In all my travels to negotiate the human network surrounding the Handler, I'd just encountered the first ray of personal leverage that I could use against him. And, frustratingly, it would no longer matter in a few hours. I'd crossed the threshold of placing the pistol in my sling. There was no going back.

But that didn't change the fact that Parvaneh would be left caring for her daughter alone. The thought was sickening.

"Then why not escape?" I asked.

"My influence grows with each passing day. With control comes modernization, and that's the greatest good I can achieve. For Langley, and the world. Taking over the Organization will be the greatest escape of all, David."

"You'll never be able to legalize it, whatever it is. It will always be a criminal enterprise."

"That's the world we live in. But that enterprise wields more power than any politician. I can prevent scores of deaths each year, create thousands of legitimate jobs, and marshal millions of dollars to the benefit of those who need it most."

"Your daughter is going to be trapped in a web of

murder and crime, Parvaneh, no matter how eloquently you try to justify it."

"If I took Langley away from the Organization, she could always be drawn back out of a sense of destiny or wealth. If I take over, there will be no role for her to step into. The seat of power has become too powerful for one person, and I intend on dispersing a position that's been centuries in the making."

"And what happens when the Handler finds out your plans?"

"I make no secret of my intentions. He can control all he wants for now. When he cedes authority to me, the power of transcendence comes with it."

Her hand slid down from the medical dressing on my shoulder to clasp my uninjured hand. A rush of heat swept through my chest as our fingers interlaced.

"Who was Langley's father?" I asked.

She smiled mournfully, glancing to the engagement ring.

"An Outfit shooter, like you. He was selected for promotion from the Complex. We met and fell in love." She looked away from the ring, her eyes drifting unfocused to the curtain behind me. "I was pregnant with Langley when he was killed on assignment."

"I'm sorry. What happened?"

"The circumstances are classified."

"Your father has never told you?"

"I've demanded to know many times. I continue demanding to this day. But when I take the throne, I'll have access to everything. And revenge sharpens with time."

I could take a pretty good guess why the Handler hadn't shared that information with her: given everything

I knew about him to date, he probably played a seminal part in the death.

I said, "I lost someone very close to me, too. A woman I was in love with."

"Recently?"

"Always."

She smiled sadly. "That's the burden we bear as survivors. I can see Langley's father in her. But I've been so alone since losing him."

I watched her eyes brim with tears, and I knew what she felt: the emotion of trying to survive, her elation upon seeing Gabriel clashing against the truth of his betrayal, the entire horrid juxtaposition ending in physical attraction for someone who reminded her of the love she'd lost.

Without a word, she leaned over my stretcher to whisper in my ear.

"So, David, do you accept my job offer?"

Then she kissed me, the hot, salty taste of her tears flowing past my lips. She pulled back, hovering inches from the .32 pistol concealed in my sling.

My decision was made.

I'd kill her father but no more; if I wasn't shot outright, I'd drop my weapon and let her take revenge on me. I looked to her green, tear-blurred pupils.

"If I survive this, Parvaneh, I'll surrender to your will."

She lifted my uninjured hand and laid a kiss across my knuckles. "The medic said you'll be fine. He'd better be right."

I watched her expression and sighed wistfully. "'The Girl from Ipanema.'"

"We met in Leblon, David. Don't get sentimental." Then she released my hand and stood. "I need to smooth things over with Micah. He reports everything to my father."

"Don't let me hold you back."

She cast a final forlorn glance across my injuries and turned, passing through the curtain and leaving me alone.

FATE

Antebellum

-Before the war

9

The plane touched down and began its howling deceleration on the Handler's airstrip as I braced myself on the stretcher. The curtain surrounding the medical area had been pulled back, revealing the otherwise nondescript interior of a cargo plane whose glow had transitioned from white to red lighting half an hour ago, just as the plane started to descend.

Now that we had landed, Parvaneh, Micah, and Reilly rose from their seats and clustered around me. Parvaneh spoke first.

"You don't have to get up. We can cover you with a parka and roll the stretcher."

She and Micah had already donned black coats, and Micah held an extra one for me. I thought about meeting the Handler like this—my angle of fire restricted to a waist-high plane of limited visibility, unable to move or pivot to influence the last bullet I'd ever fire.

"I can walk."

She looked to Reilly for approval.

"How far does he need to move, ma'am?" Micah

looked up sharply, and Reilly corrected himself. "Sorry—I don't need to know, I'm not asking. If David feels his pain is manageable, then he'll be able to walk."

The plane came to a complete halt with a final quaking lurch of brakes, and Reilly assisted me to a standing position. I fought to keep my left arm motionless within the sling, but the pain was immense. Unwilling to risk a deadening of my reflexes at this crucial time, I'd refused further painkillers. As a result, my broken left humerus once again felt like jagged bones grating against one another.

Micah draped a parka over my shoulders and leaned in so Reilly couldn't hear. "Don't worry. You're not going far."

I nodded, watching the ramp lower at the rear of the aircraft.

Darkness lay beyond, and a single figure approached. I wouldn't be lucky enough for the Handler to board, I knew, and assumed the approaching form would be Sage.

But instead of the redheaded woman it was an Asian man—tall, broad-shouldered, long hair combed back into a low bun. Drastic eyebrows belied a face that was perfectly composed, relaxed even.

He stopped before Parvaneh, speaking in a deep voice rich with formality. "Welcome back, ma'am. I speak for everyone when I say that—"

"Where is he, Ishway?"

"Waiting for you inside, ma'am." He held a hand out toward me, and within his gloved palm was a familiar pair of blacked-out goggles.

Parvaneh shook her head. "David has spilled blood for this Organization and saved my life. He's not an outsider anymore."

"Yes, ma'am." The goggles vanished back into Ishway's coat pocket. He looked to Reilly and said, "Thank you for your service to the Organization. Everything that has transpired from the time you left your departure airfield in Brazil until you return to it is classified. You are not to speak of it again, under any circumstances. Anyone who inquires in any way must be reported to your Outfit chain of command at once."

Reilly nodded his understanding and Ishway concluded, "You are to remain on the plane. You'll be on your way as soon as the parcel is offloaded."

Then he turned and led Parvaneh, Micah, and me toward the ramp. I was uncertain what he meant by "parcel" until I saw two additional men entering the plane and taking possession of the body bag containing Gabriel's remains.

As we walked past them I glanced at the weapons slung over their shoulders, unable to stop myself any more than a lecher eyeing cleavage. They carried shorty M4s, 10.5-inch free-floating barrels and reflex sights that were probably good up to one hundred meters. No uniform consistency beyond civilian jackets worn under miniature plate carriers, bare except for extra rifle magazines. Varying degrees of beard growth and hair length— no one gave a shit what these two looked like as long as they could shoot, and do it well, and they paid us no mind as they prepared to lift Gabriel's corpse.

We stepped off the ramp and into the freezing cold air, the unzipped parka over my shoulders doing little to ward off the chill but keeping my arm sling—and the pistol within it—readily accessible.

Our surroundings were only vaguely visible, with thick fog transmuting the first light of dawn into a dull luminescence. I looked down the runway that disappeared into the mist, seeing a straight strip of pavement devoid of markings or lights. There was no control tower. Glancing back at the plane, I saw it had no exterior lights on. The tail appeared a black shape in the darkness, and there was no way for me to see if it had a registration number. I caught Micah watching me closely, trailing a few steps behind and to the side.

Looking forward, I saw a murky forest drenched in fog. Towering pines ascended into a shapeless, smoky mist that hovered overhead, and as with my first visit, the smell of wet pine took hold once we passed beyond the fumes of plane exhaust. Once again, it was both cold and humid, but there was no snow at this early date in January; that combination of facts would have been ideal for narrowing weather patterns of the Pacific Northwest to pinpoint the Mist Palace's location.

But I was past that point now, I reminded myself.

A chain-link fence with barbed wire appeared through the trees, the only portal through it a small building that we approached. What lay beyond the fence looked like a resort in the mountains: buildings were visible, to be sure, but only in hints amid the forest. Whoever had built the structures must have taken incredible measures to leave as many trees standing as possible.

I watched Ishway's and Parvaneh's breath billowing white in the early morning air, and tried to subdue the limp brought on by a nagging irritation in my right knee.

My mind was churning with the magnitude of my situation. I had survived my first meeting with the Handler against all odds, with the help of the young Somali woman now on the other side of the world; I'd returned from an impossible set of circumstances in Rio after getting shot for my efforts; now I'd arrived at the Mist Palace once more, with a weapon on my person and the distance closing between me and my long-sought quarry. I wouldn't see the sunrise that morning no matter what I did or didn't do. The only question was whether I took the Handler out with me.

We stopped at the building's front door, and Ishway swiped a panel on the wall with a card attached to a lanyard around his neck. With a beep, the door clicked open—just like at the Complex—and we entered the warm, brightly lit space.

It was a security checkpoint.

Two agents were in the room, both wearing black outdoor clothing and holstered Glocks. They had the stature and bearing of career security agents, and they straightened when they saw Parvaneh enter.

The room was set up much like a TSA screening checkpoint, with a conveyor belt leading into a scanner, a table and chairs for individual searches, and, in the center of the room, a walk-through metal detector.

Parvaneh and Ishway walked through without a blip, while Micah remained behind me. I hesitated.

"Step through," an agent said.

I did, and the screeching, high-pitched beep of the detector protested.

The agent directed me to stop, then ran a wand between my legs and around my torso, front and back. Its only warbling chime came in the vicinity of my splint.

"I'm sorry, sir," he said. "We're going to have to do a physical search."

The other agent stepped forward and held my wrist with one hand, sliding his palm against my inside forearm and toward the pistol.

I stepped back. "This isn't a fashion statement. My arm is broken."

He was unrepentant. "Sir, I'll need you to have a seat and let us remove the sling. You're not stepping foot out of this building until we do."

I looked past his pointed finger at the table. If I propped my elbow on it and they untied my sling, even momentarily, the pistol would come clattering to the surface. I hesitated, my neck ablaze with the guilt of getting caught. As I took a step toward the table and my mind raced to consider alternative options, Parvaneh spoke.

"I would be dead right now if David hadn't laid down his life for me. If either of you touch him again, *you're* going to need splints—"

"Please," Micah interceded. "Mr. Rivers is wearing a splint constructed of aluminum. The nature of his injuries necessitates an exception to policy, and he has been under direct supervision since being shot. Call it in."

The agents maintained their unapologetic poise, but one spoke into a radio.

"Positive metal on Mr. Rivers. Micah requests exception to policy, citing physical injury and metallic splint."

"*Standby.*"

My heart hammered as we waited for a response. Looking up, I saw a camera in the corner of the ceiling. I wondered who was staring back at me, deciding whether to let me pass.

"*Exception to policy approved. Send Mr. Rivers through.*"

"Copy." He looked to us and nodded. "Thank you for your patience."

Parvaneh led the way as we passed through the far door and into the early morning light.

* * *

We approached a chain-link cage whose gate only slid open after the door behind us locked into place. We continued forward, and I saw that what I thought had been a resort was actually a vast fortress.

A clear-cut swath of land extended three meters to the next fence. The ground on either side of the footpath was a flat, muddy expanse of perfectly even dirt extending in both directions. Metal poles rose at varying intervals above the opposite fence, topped with inscrutable black boxes that surely contained cameras, thermal optics, and motion sensors. I noted that the width of this no-man's land was insufficient to be seen through the tree canopy. The gate behind us rumbled shut and clicked into place, and an identical gate to our front slid open.

I looked up as we walked into the compound; the area was almost completely shielded from overhead view by towering hardwood treetops. Even if the trees weren't present, an aerial observer could fly a hundred feet over-head without seeing anything through the haze of mist.

We passed into the fort's interior, where dim solar lights in the ground murkily illuminated the paved trails between the buildings. My heart rate rose with each foot-fall toward the Handler.

At a trail juncture, Ishway said, "This way, ma'am. He's waiting for you in the garden."

Parvaneh stopped abruptly. "The garden?"

"Yes, ma'am."

She turned to Micah. "What did you tell him?"

"Only the truth," he replied, his voice unyielding in the darkness.

Parvaneh regarded him with an expression I couldn't read in the dim light. "Very well. Let's go."

A turn down the paved trail took us toward an eerie sight—a fifteen-foot stone wall topped with concertina wire that seemed a dominating fixture amid the fort's interior. Its walls extended a great distance through the forest, with additional trees rising from inside it. It was a fortress within a fortress, a seeming prison contradicted by the lack of a roof.

I couldn't make the connection between that sight and any discernable definition of a garden, but our guide led us to a cast iron gate with three guards at each side.

They were clean-shaven, wearing stocking caps and unbuttoned overcoats. While they stood in a range of postures, each man watched me with the single-minded focus of a police dog awaiting an order to run down a fleeing suspect.

This is where I get frisked, I thought. This is where they catch me.

But instead, two of the guards opened the gate.

"Ms. Parvaneh and Mr. Rivers only," Ishway said. "Micah, you are to wait outside."

Micah slowed, processing this order with a sense of shock betrayed by a stutter-step toward the gate.

"There must be some mistake," Micah said.

"There's not."

Parvaneh swept inside, and I struggled to keep pace with my knee on fire and left humerus smoldering. Looking back, I saw Micah watching us with Ishway at his side as the guards closed the gate, locking Parvaneh and me inside. I caught up to her and took in my first glimpse of what lay within the walls.

The interior was stunningly landscaped, more botanical garden than anything else. Ground lighting cast a palette of soft pastels onto the plants. The path beneath our feet turned to a trail of interconnected flat stone pieces that meandered through tranquil ponds, the landscape beset by a vast array of plants and trees that looked strangely exotic for what I presumed was the Pacific Northwest.

I asked, "Why does he want to meet us outside? It's freezing."

"He's expecting a fight."

"What does that have to do with the garden?"

"He's unwilling to meet alone because of his fetish for bodyguards. But he seeks to isolate his organization from heated personal debates with his daughter."

"I don't follow."

"Only his closest protectors have already seen the full range of drama in a very complicated relationship between me and him. This is the only place where he can minimize the number of witnesses."

"You didn't do anything wrong. Why should there be a confrontation?"

Her eyes directed ahead, she didn't respond. I reached in my sling to position the pistol back on the inside of my injured wrist, wincing with the effort.

Even under such bizarre circumstances, the pain in my knee and gunshot wounds dissipating amid the exhilaration of my imminent and final confrontation with the Handler, I was moved by the beauty of my surroundings. Empty benches overlooked views of fountains and boulder arrangements. As we passed over a footbridge arching across a stretch of flowing water, I looked past the ornate guiderails to see enormous fish gliding beneath the surface. A long, serpentine shape dwarfed them all as it sliced through their ranks.

During that walk I thought not about the totality of my life, but the finality of my death.

And that's all it came down to. After all the late-night ruminations of suicide, the close calls while parachuting from buildings and hunting other men, the desire to avenge Karma or save Ian or pursue adrenaline rushes to the very boundaries of existence, it came down to this: at the moment everything was on the line, I shut out my surroundings, everything in my past and the whisper of a future with Parvaneh that would never be, and compartmentalized my life to a single-minded focus on pointing my gun at the Handler's face and pulling the trigger.

There would be no vengeful last words, no explanation of justice sewn or retribution claimed. I would extend my one functioning arm, the tiny pistol announced only by a small plume of smoke and an impossibly quiet *pop* before his body fell where he stood, likely striking the ground only a moment before I joined him.

Pulling the trigger would be my last act in life. There would be no time for a second shot. But one was all I needed.

A fleeting tribute, perhaps, but it was nothing if not fitting. Onward I had trudged, marching toward his distant figure, until now, when it would soon appear before me for the second and final time. No matter how empty an achievement my revenge had become in the path required to attain it, this was the last chance I'd ever get.

I unexpectedly remembered the words of the Somali woman: *Giants are not slain at the end of golden roads.*

She'd saved my life once already.

He is going to test you, and when the moment seems perfect to complete your revenge, that is the very time you must not do it.

But I'd already seen his test, passing up on the opportunity to attack him in the death chamber where the Indian had been electrocuted.

We approached a bamboo pavilion on a small hill, and while I was certain that another search lay ahead, I saw two figures standing casually within, waiting for us to arrive at the stone staircase leading up to them.

One of them was unmistakably the Handler.

I could tell it was him even from a distance, his tall, lean form and shaved silver hair distinguishable at once. At his side I recognized Racegun, who surely still carried his modified 1911 pistol. He would respond quickly—but I would be quicker.

We hit the bottom of the stairs and began ascending. The pain in my knee flared as the two figures appeared over the edge above me.

Without Racegun's presence I could have risked an inclined shot as I ascended. But with two steps to go, I planned to close the distance and come to a standing, stable position from which to fire the one bullet that would topple a dictator.

I climbed the second to last step, then took in the odd positioning of him and his guard. They seemed to be standing around some central installment of interest, and as I took the final step onto the platform, I saw what it was.

On his knees, facing us, arms tied behind his back as he looked at me with eyes red, tear-blurred, but full of hatred, was Ian.

He was unshaven, his left cheekbone swollen in a dark

purple bruise, the veins on his balding temples standing out in stark relief. I studied him as I walked forward—I'd warned him, and he'd gotten caught anyway. My situation had become infinitely more complicated in a split second, and yet Ian's eyes were unapologetic.

Parvaneh and I stood level with the Handler and his guard, the bound captive kneeling between us. Parvaneh exploded, "What is the meaning of this?"

I could take the shot from where I stood.

But to what end? It would no longer save Ian. He would die anyway; we both would.

The Handler spoke in a calm, measured tone, his voice easing around the syllables with patience. "A conspiracy between two men who plotted to kill me."

The prophecy had been fulfilled, I realized, and now he would sever the bond between Parvaneh and me, killing the remaining two conspirators in the process.

He held a long arm toward Ian. "The architect, Avner Ian Greenberg."

The Handler pointed to me, amber eyes meeting mine for the briefest of seconds, his face shaking with the slight tremor I'd seen the first time we'd met. "And David Clayton Rivers. The assassin."

Parvaneh's head swung to me, her eyes frozen in a profoundly confused stare. "David, is this true?"

"Absolutely." I looked to the Handler. "Now tell her why."

He continued, "They served on a paramilitary team that turned against us."

"Tell her how you sentenced that team to death for serving you."

"Then David lied to infiltrate the Outfit, killing his partner in the process."

"Tell her how you turned that partner into a traitor to his own team. And tell her," I nearly shouted, "how you killed the woman I loved."

His head bowed deeply in a serene nod. "Yes. I gave the order."

"Because they knew too much? They did everything you asked."

"The interconnectedness of life sometimes has unintended consequences—"

"How does it feel to see your daughter again? Because I'll never see the woman you took away from me."

Parvaneh said, "Father, you've earned many legitimate enemies. David can be spared and hired. He must be—I've given him my word of honor. Langley would have been an orphan"—the word cracked as it left her lips—"without him. And I will not stand by and watch my savior be killed."

The Handler's glinting golden eyes were not upon his daughter but me, the angled bridge of his nose defiant against the symmetry of his features. "Then your savior shall watch Ian die. I cannot permit a resurrection of the conspiracy between them."

"Very well," Parvaneh conceded.

I could take the shot from where I stood. But in that moment, the Handler's death would accomplish nothing but condemn an innocent friend to die.

I had to find a way to save Ian.

"No," I said. "I trade my life for his. You've got your assassin—now release Ian. I want Parvaneh's word that he will live, because yours"—I took a breath to calm the surge of anger looking at the Handler's face imparted—"means nothing to me."

The Handler shook his head. "It is honor that assured

our Organization's continued survival. Not leniency. Be grateful you are not meeting the same fate."

"Be grateful I saved your daughter after everything you've done. I brought her back to you; now you can accept my life in exchange. Parvaneh, do this for me."

She said, "I'm sorry, David. It wasn't your friend who saved my life, but you. This is the way it has to be."

Ian spoke grimly. "Don't die along with me, David. I was never meant to be the last surviving member of the team—you were."

The Handler lifted his outstretched fingers toward Ian, and Racegun set an anticipatory hand on his pistol. I couldn't force the Handler's decision, I realized.

But Parvaneh could.

Reaching inside my sling in a swift movement, I pulled the .32 from its hiding place and pressed the barrel against my own temple.

The response was so immediate that by the time the gun touched my scalp, Racegun had his pistol aimed at my face while simultaneously shifting to block the Handler from view in a single fleeting step. The Handler touched Racegun's arm and pushed him sideways and out of his line of sight, watching me once more. His eyes were fixated on my gun.

By then I was speaking quickly. "Parvaneh, you will have Ian pardoned or I blow my head off. Three."

Parvaneh's face steeled with resolution as she turned to the Handler.

"Father, spare them both. You already have Roshan's blood on your hands—"

I suddenly remembered my final confrontation with Caspian in Somalia, yelling at his bloodied figure on the hilltop. *That was your scout, wasn't it? In the desert I asked if*

*Sergio recruited you. You said it was an Iranian named
Roshan.*

"Two."

"—if the blood of my savior is spilt, by his hand or
yours, I take Langley and walk away from this organization forever."

My heart was hammering at an unsustainable rate,
feeling like it would explode as I watched the Handler's
face. A vast depth of intellect lay therein, but I had seen
his instability firsthand and was dismayed now to observe
neither fear nor surprise in his expression.

"One."

"Very well," the Handler said. "They both shall live."

I dropped the .32 before I got shot in the face.

The pistol clattered to the ground and Racegun was
upon me in an instant, forcing me to my knees in front of
Ian and placing his barrel to my head. My collective
injuries exploded in pain, causing a total-body convulsion
of agony—the least of my concerns at present.

Parvaneh snatched the .32 off the ground.

The Handler stepped forward, holding out his hand to
take the gun from her.

"You're afraid I'd use this on you?" she asked, her voice
indignant.

He kept his hand out, not speaking until she thrust the
tiny pistol into it. Once she did, he examined it with an
expression of mild fascination that faded as quickly as it
appeared. His long fingers spun shut over the weapon like
a spider shielding its prey from escape.

"I'm afraid, Parvaneh," he said, lowering the gun to his
side with his eyes canted downward, "that you would use
it on David."

"What does that mean?"

"He and his friend are alive. I have given you what you asked. Leave it at that."

"What does that mean?" she repeated, more loudly than before.

The Handler spoke mournfully. "My hands aren't stained with Roshan's blood." He nodded toward Ian. "His are."

Then he cast his gaze upon me. "And David's."

Parvaneh's face darkened, her green eyes blazing with rage. "TELL ME!"

I remembered being in the basement of the team house as Ophie tortured Luka, who was screaming that he didn't kill Caspian, that it was the Iranian. I leaned over to Matz and asked, *Who's the Iranian?*

And Matz's reply: *He's dead already.*

The Iranian killed by Boss's team before I met them, a man named Roshan who faked Caspian's death to recruit him into the Outfit, and the father of Parvaneh's daughter —all three were the same person.

And Ian and I were about to bear the consequences.

The Handler said, "That's why I sentenced their team to death, Parvaneh. They killed Roshan. Ian located and kidnapped him. The others tortured him and cut off his head."

She shook her head. "That's a lie."

"I've never lied to you, Parvaneh."

"You're a fucking *liar!*" she yelled.

"Since his death, I could have invented a thousand easy answers to ease your pain. I have not told you until now because when I speak to you, since the moment you were born, I speak the truth."

Parvaneh lowered her eyes to mine, her stare cutting through me. "David?"

"I had nothing to do with that," I said. "I hadn't even met them—"

She unleashed a moaning gasp of pain, doubling over before she stood again.

I said, "Parvaneh, they thought he killed their teammate. In a defection scheme ordered by your father—"

"Stop it," she cried. "David, just stop."

The Handler stepped forward and took her in his arms. The embrace lasted a second before Parvaneh shrugged him off and stepped back, shattered. She understood the implications of me smuggling a pistol into that meeting yet had fought to save me anyway—for a time.

But the Handler's words had broken her.

She spoke shakily now, her incredible resolve gone. "I always vowed I would kill those responsible for Roshan's death—now I've saved you both. And I've got the rest of my life to regret that."

Then she looked to the Handler and said, "What happens to them now is not my concern. I never want to see David again."

He turned his hand upward, showing her the .32 pistol in his palm.

"You will not, my dear. The problem that has been plaguing us requires both a bond of loyalty and a measure of collateral. For the first time, we have both: David has just passed up a chance to kill me in order to risk dying for his friend."

Parvaneh nodded, and then dropped her gaze to the ground.

What were they talking about?

I looked to her. "I swear to you, Parvaneh, I had nothing to do with Roshan." Then I swung my eyes to the

Handler. "But *you*, motherfucker, killed the love of my life when you killed Karma."

His eyes remained on his daughter.

"Leave us. Go be with Langley now. She's waiting for you."

"Parvaneh," I said, "he's hidden the truth until he could use it to manipulate you. But you know me, and we've felt the same pain. Don't let him win."

Standing in the presence of Ian, the Handler, and myself, each of us suddenly bearing some role in the death of her child's father, she no longer knew what to believe.

She took a few short steps backward, almost to the edge of the pavilion. She looked confused, lost in pain, and with a sharp turn that spared not a sideways glance at her father, or me, she walked off the platform, down the stairs, and into the garden.

I wanted to yell after her, but it was no use—the last traces of her footsteps vanished along the trail.

Ian's voice was hoarse, raw with hatred. "Why didn't Roshan just tell my team that Caspian was alive?"

The Handler placed the tips of his index and middle fingers thoughtfully upon his upper lip before replying. "The Outfit screens for people who would face torture and death before compromising secrets. David knows that well by now."

I jerked my head toward him before the barrel against my skull forced my view back down. "Why let me return to America and join the Outfit if you always knew I was on Boss's team?"

"I never stop people from revenge. I lay a path and wait at the end of it."

Ian looked to me with contempt. "I don't know how

you got a gun next to him, David, but you should have used it."

"I did use it, you ungrateful bastard."

"You should've killed him when you had the chance."

"Well next time I'll let you get smoked."

"There's not going to be a next time. We're both dead anyway."

"Gentlemen," the Handler interrupted, "do not overestimate your resourcefulness, or my ignorance. David brought a gun in my immediate proximity for one reason alone: because I wanted him to."

Then he pointed an arm toward my face, the .32 a splinter of metal in his long fingers. With the barrel leveled at my head, he pulled the trigger.

A hollow *click*.

My mind launched back to Micah's intervention at the security checkpoint. *The nature of his injuries necessitates an exception to policy, and he has been under direct supervision since being shot. Call it in.*

I shook my head bitterly. "Micah?"

"You were unconscious in the plane for some time, David."

"So that's why you agreed to spare my life in front of Parvaneh. You thought I was about to die in a failed assassination attempt."

"The greatest protection," he responded, "is seeing what people do when they think you are unaware of their plans."

Ian closed his eyes, lowering his head in a concession of rueful finality.

The Handler continued, "My apologies, gentlemen. Your plan to kill me was admirable given your resources, but far from original. And now you are both in my immediate service."

Behind me, Racegun said, "She's just left the garden, sir."

"What happened here tonight will never be spoken of again. Bring David to my chamber at once. Ian to a cell." The Handler walked past us and off the platform, checking his watch.

I heard bushes rustling below the pavilion, followed by a rush of footsteps ascending the stairs before a group of security men appeared on the platform—four? A half dozen? They wore camouflage fatigues and carried suppressed weapons, their night vision devices flipped upward on tactical helmets.

Ian stared at me vacantly.

I said, "I will get you out of this, Ian."

Then we were hoisted upright by the security team, separated, and carried out of the garden.

10

My left arm felt like a drill bit was being pushed through it as the pain of being strapped to the chair mounted. Once more the blacked-out goggles blocked my vision, but between the Handler's order for me to be delivered to his chamber and his security men strapping me to a chair for the second time, I felt certain I once again occupied the throne where the Indian had died.

And in the short wait before the Handler's arrival, I reflected upon his genius with a curious sense of disbelief.

The Handler had known I carried a pistol toward him, but he couldn't possibly have foreseen that I would put that weapon to my own head. Yet in the wake of a single element disrupting his entire plan, he had deftly manipulated the situation to his advantage nonetheless.

By finally revealing the truth about Roshan's death, the Handler had turned Parvaneh away from me, broken the bond between us that was forged when I saved her life, and gained her ambivalence if not outright complicity to send me to my death. He had seamlessly restored order to his world at the expense of his daughter, Ian, and myself. What he had in mind for his next move across the chessboard of human actors, I had no idea.

But I knew with great certainty that something worse awaited.

A door opened somewhere behind me. I heard his unhurried footfalls approaching and directed my blacked-out goggles toward the sound as it arced around my side and came to a stop at my front.

His fingers grazed my bare scalp, the smell of cloves reaching my nostrils just as the elastic band of the goggles slid over the back of my head.

I squinted with the sudden light, seeing his face before mine as he leaned down to appraise me. But as I blinked to clear my vision, I saw that I was not in the chamber where the Indian was executed.

Instead, the view beyond the Handler's gaunt face was a colossal, lavishly appointed room. High gray walls led to a low, ornate wooden desk adorned with computer monitors.

Seeing that I wasn't in the electric chair, I allowed myself a gasp of pain.

His palm alighted on my right shoulder as he said, "Thank you, David, for saving my daughter in Brazil."

He lifted his hand and ran it over his close-cropped silver hair, then began to walk in a methodical circle around me.

"Fucking *really*? That's all you have to say?"

He continued circling my chair, his face creasing into a knowing smile as he crossed my view. "Do you know what truly troubles you, David? You hate what I represent: order. Balance. *Unity*. I am but the embodiment of every-thing you lack. You are addicted to chaos, to uncertainty. You are struck by the meaninglessness of life so often and so violently that you resent everyone not so afflicted. And I am the manifestation of total control."

"You're a mass murderer who considers yourself a messiah. That's the manifestation of total insanity."

"You have demonstrated considerable tenacity since you joined your last team, David. Please do not mar your credibility or waste our precious moments together with petty insults. I have a war to conduct, which is one of the more enjoyable aspects of my position. Given that the opposition tried to kill my daughter, it will be ecstasy. Gabriel has a surprising number of living relatives to attempt what he did."

He crossed behind my chair again, and I glanced upward to see that the ceiling was lined not with crown molding but a peculiar red pipe standing in stark contrast to the rest of the room. *What the hell*?

"You can't punish a dead man," I said.

"Murdering families in spectacular fashion does not serve to rebuke dead traitors, David. It serves to convince those who haven't betrayed the Organization to remain loyal."

"You're missing the bigger picture."

"I highly doubt that."

"Gabriel must've known you'd kill his entire family for betrayal."

"Most assuredly."

"Then what did the other side offer that was more fearsome by comparison? You know Ribeiro's man Agustin was on the kill team they sent after us. No one else on the kill team was present at the meeting, but Agustin was. The attempt on Parvaneh's life is a part of something bigger, and Ribeiro can't be the only player."

"I came to my own conclusions prior to your return

from Brazil. But they don't concern you. So let us instead discuss the terms of your upcoming employment."

"I saved your daughter. You owe me some answers first."

He stopped in front of me, tilting his head. "I thought we had covered everything in the garden, David. What is it that you are still unclear about?"

"Clearly it was you speaking during my interview from the Outfit."

He nodded, the angle of his skewed nose casting a bobbing shadow across his face.

"Why mention my father?"

"I couldn't help myself, David. You have to admit, your pedigree is somewhat ironic given your chosen profession."

He began walking again, circling me with steady footfalls like the ticking of a grandfather clock.

"You must have put Boss's team under surveillance as soon as Roshan was killed."

"I could not risk letting them escape after such a transgression."

"But you could risk letting them finish your dirty work before you murdered them all?"

"As I told you at our first meeting, David, my role is to maintain balance. Harmony is not preserved by completely sacrificing the professional for the personal or vice versa, no matter how tantalizing the prospect may seem at times."

"Why quote them in my interview? Why toy with me?"

"To get the wheels turning, of course, before I paired you with Caspian. How could I not, David, knowing I had the two of you from the same team, both clinging to your lies in the aftermath of their loss..."

"Why test me if you planned on killing me anyway?"

"It was not you I tested, David. I expected a single survivor from Somalia. I just thought it would be Caspian."

I managed a tight grin and said, "Sorry to disappoint you."

"To the contrary, I believe the mission went rather well. For a man in my position, unexpected outcomes are inevitable, at times."

"Heavy is the head that wears the crown of highly enriched uranium?"

Upon realizing Caspian had told me the contents of the case from Somalia, the Handler stopped walking for several seconds. Then he continued his stroll before responding, "Most men of sound mind would be glad that substance was removed from the world stage."

"As a key component for building a nuclear weapon, sure. But I have trouble believing you plan on using it for a paperweight."

His lips pursed in solidarity before his expression righted itself. He circled back behind me.

"Of course, we have obtained the militia commander's account of what transpired between you and him on the hilltop in Somalia. Including the fact that Caspian had not yet been shot and"—he crossed my front, wincing slightly as if the notion brought him pain—"you asked for an AK-47 to be left behind. That information would be of great interest to many at the Complex, including Sergio—"

"I think we're beyond threats at this point."

"Now, now, David, we are never *beyond* threats. Counterbalanced with incentive, threats keep balance, order. I could threaten to inform the Outfit that you killed a beloved operator on your excursion to Africa, and then deliver you to meet their justice. Or I could incentivize you by keeping your secret and leaving open the possibility of what you want most in this world."

"Your death?"

"That is not what you want most, David. You want to continue participating in missions. That is your lifeline, as it were, your tenuous grasp to remaining alive by facing death."

"Remaining alive isn't worth being in your service."

"You are no longer a servant. Now you are a slave, and Ian's life hangs in the balance."

"You're going to kill him no matter what I do or don't do."

"To the contrary, killing him serves no purpose but closing a loop that is satisfied equally well by his captivity. I would much prefer to employ him. He successfully evaded my people's efforts to locate him for some time now. Otherwise I would not have had to resort to luring him to the airport."

"You're lying."

"I am not."

"You could have lured him any way you wanted."

"Ah, but you were the only bait that has worked. He had four separate operatives positively identify you in the lounge before he risked exposing himself. Prior to that he evaded my men's surveillance efforts every time he left the house of your former paramilitary team. He has a skill set I could use, and I intend on doing just that."

"You just staged an elaborate puppet show to manipulate your daughter into complying with your master plan. You'll understand if I choose not to believe you."

"I should mention the alternative to your compliance

is watching Ian tortured to death in front of you, right now, using the most imaginative methods at my people's disposal that will make Roshan's and Luka's deaths seem benevolent. Surely you would prefer my job offer."

"You're talking about what you said in the garden—the problem that requires collateral."

"I am."

"What did that mean?"

He came to a stop before me, ending the ticking clock of his footsteps. Turning to face my chair, he leaned down, lowering his eerie amber eyes to mine.

He spoke quietly, methodically, in a sickly amused tone.

"You've tried to kill me once, David Rivers." A smile twisted his lips. "I need you to try it again."

* * *

Check out the next in series, Vengeance Calling! Continue reading for a sample.

Sign up for the Reader List and be the first to know about new releases and special offers from former Green Beret and USA Today bestselling author, Jason Kasper.

Join Jason Kasper's Reader List at Jason-Kasper.com

As a thank you for signing up, you'll receive a free copy of The Ranger Objective: An American Mercenary Short Story.

VENGEANCE CALLING: AMERICAN MERCENARY #4

David Rivers' luck has finally run out.

He's been condemned to certain death as a deep cover agent.

But his new mission reveals an unlikely ally with one shared goal: the death of David's greatest enemy.

A brilliant assassination plot is already underway. And the final element is trapped amid the firestorm of a civil war in Myanmar.

To kill his opponent and free his only surviving teammate, David will have to survive impossible odds—odds that he's determined to beat, no matter the cost.

As a perilous journey unfolds, David learns that appearances aren't as they seem, and no loyalties are absolute.

He finds himself forced to choose between two great evils —with his only friend's life hanging in the balance.

Get your copy today at Jason-Kasper.com

ALSO BY JASON KASPER

American Mercenary Series

Greatest Enemy
Offer of Revenge
Dark Redemption
Vengeance Calling
The Suicide Cartel
Terminal Objective

Shadow Strike Series

The Enemies of My Country

Spider Heist Thrillers

The Spider Heist
The Sky Thieves
The Manhattan Job

Standalone Thriller

Her Dark Silence

Want to stay in the loop?

Sign up to be the FIRST to learn about new releases. Plus get newsletter only bonus content for FREE.

As a thank you for signing up, you'll receive a free copy of *The Ranger Objective.* Join today at **Jason-Kasper.com/newsletter**

ACKNOWLEDGMENTS

Once again, I owe my gratitude to an outstanding—and ever growing—group of people for their massive help in the third installment of the David Rivers series.

For the past decade-plus of writing, of which only the last year and a half have been in the public eye, my sister Julie has been the only person to view the initial draft of anything I've written. Her eye for recognizing potential, or lack thereof, in the formative stage of every scene and story has been invaluable in guiding my hand through countless revisions. As my content editor and as my sister, I can't thank her enough.

My beta readers deserve the majority of the credit for every book I write. Each of them reviewed an early manuscript of this book and thoughtfully weighed in on what I needed to improve, bridging the gap between my good intentions and often disastrous initial presentation. I gave myself two weeks between receiving their feedback and delivering the manuscript to my editor, and ended up needing every minute of that time to integrate their input.

They are: Ben B, Bob W (Go Navy!), Codename: Duchess, Clay, David "Doc" B (RLTW!), Dean F, Derek, Gwendolyn, Howard, Jamie B, Janet, Joe C, Jon Suttle, Joseph "Ishway" Iesué, JT (THS!), Kelly T, Mickey J, Mike T, Tim C, Timothy D, and Wilson G.

Additionally, I owe a huge thanks to five specialized beta readers: my medical advisory team, Aaron Cestaro, Gypsy113D, and Randy, as well as my cultural and language advisors, Nick and Clarice L.

Mark B of Armormax provided technical consult, and Joseph Iesué and Stephanie L contributed the names "Ishway" and "Sage" in this book—and there will be much more of both characters in the next one!

I owe an additional debt to Ranger vet, author, and pastor Jeff Struecker. In 1999, I was a high school student reading about Jeff in *Blackhawk Down*; in 2001, I was an Army basic trainee seeing Jeff's uniform on display at the Infantry Museum in Fort Benning, Georgia; and in 2018, I was an author consulting him for this book. His feedback enriched elements of this story far beyond my own capabilities. For that, and for inspiring myself and many other future, current, and former Rangers, I will be forever grateful.

As a professional editor, Cara Quinlan has been making sense of my feeble attempts at grammatical propriety for three books running. If she can stomach any more of my literary ineptitude, she can consider herself hired for the next three and beyond—I don't seem to be getting any better at English as I go, and her painstaking efforts have greatly elevated each manuscript that crosses her desk. Thanks for putting up with me at every turn, Cara.

Finally, my beautiful and long-suffering wife Amy deserves more recognition than I can provide. Her unyielding support of my writing has endured since the moment we met and continues to this day. What started as her demand that I spend my first six months after leaving the Army writing full time has turned into over a year and counting—without her, I would have been unable to complete one book, much less three, and given her constant encouragement, I'm certain that many more works lie ahead.

ABOUT THE AUTHOR

Jason Kasper is the USA Today bestselling author of the Spider Heist, American Mercenary, and Shadow Strike thriller series. Before his writing career he served in the US Army, beginning as a Ranger private and ending as a Green Beret captain. Jason is a West Point graduate and a veteran of the Afghanistan and Iraq wars, and was an avid ultramarathon runner, skydiver, and BASE jumper, all of which inspire his fiction.

Never miss a new release! Sign up for the Reader List at Jason-Kasper.com/newsletter

Join the Facebook Reader Group for the latest updates: facebook.com/groups/JasonKasper

Contact info:
Jason-Kasper.com
Jason@Jason-Kasper.com

twitter.com/kasperauthor
instagram.com/kasperauthor

Printed in Great Britain
by Amazon